Published by LITTLE SIMON, a division of SIMON & SCHUSTER, INC.
Simon & Schuster Building, 1230 Avenue of the Americas,
New York, New York 10020

LITTLE SIMON and colophon are trademarks of Simon & Schuster, Inc.
10 9 8 7
ISBN 0–671–44463–8
81–82431

Color separations by
Newsele Litho Ltd., Milan, Italy

Printed in Hong Kong by South China Printing Co.

Design by Dave Nash

For permission to include copyright material
acknowledgement and thanks for their help and courtesy
are due to the following publishers and authors:
Doubleday & Company Inc. for *The Patchwork Quilt*
from "A Necklace of Raindrops" by Joan Aiken. Copyright © 1968 by Joan Aiken;
Charles Scribner's Sons for *Pix Pax Pox*
from "The Bear That Liked Hugging People"
by Ruth Ainsworth and Anthony Maitland,
Text copyright © 1976 by Ruth Ainsworth;
Margaret Mahy and J. M. Dent & Sons for *The Kings of the Broom Cupboard*
from "The Second Margaret Mahy Story Book".
Reprinted by permission of Helen Hoke Associates;
Faber & Faber Ltd for *Tim Rabbit and the Scissors* from
"The Adventures of No Ordinary Rabbit" by Alison Uttley;
Coward, McCann & Geoghegan, Inc. for *The Elephant and the Bad Baby*
from "The Elephant and the Bad Baby" by Elfrida Vipont.
Copyright © 1969 by Elfrida Vipont.
All other stories in this book are retold from traditional sources
by Linda Yeatman and in this version are © Kingfisher Books Ltd
except *The Selfish Giant* by Oscar Wilde
which is reprinted in the original version.

A Treasury of BEDTIME STORIES

ILLUSTRATED BY HILDA OFFEN

A LITTLE SIMON BOOK
Published by Simon & Schuster, Inc., New York

Contents

Goldilocks
and the Three Bears

Once upon a time there were three bears who lived in a house in the forest. There was a great big father bear, a middle-sized mother bear and a tiny baby bear.

One morning, their breakfast porridge was too hot to eat, so they decided to go for a walk in the forest. While they were out, a little girl called Goldilocks came through the trees and found their house. She knocked on the door and, as there was no answer, she pushed it open and went inside.

In front of her was a table with three chairs, one large chair, one middle-sized chair and one small chair. On the table were three bowls of porridge, one large bowl, one middle-sized bowl and one small bowl – and three spoons.

Goldilocks was hungry and the porridge looked good, so she sat in the great big chair, picked up the large spoon and tried some of the porridge from the big bowl. But the chair was very big and very hard, the spoon was heavy and the porridge too hot.

Goldilocks jumped off quickly and went over to the middle-sized chair. But this chair was far too soft, and when she tried the porridge from the middle-sized bowl it was too cold. So she went over to the little chair and picked up the smallest spoon and tried some of the porridge from the tiny bowl.

This time it was neither too hot nor too cold. It was just right – and so delicious that she ate it all up. But she was too heavy for the little chair and it broke in pieces under her weight.

Next Goldilocks went upstairs, where she found three beds. There was a great big bed, a middle-sized bed and a tiny little bed. By now she was feeling rather tired, so she climbed into the big bed and lay down. The big bed was very hard and far too big. Then she tried the middle-sized bed, but that was far too soft, so she climbed into the tiny little bed. It was neither too hard nor too soft. In fact, it felt just right, all cosy and warm, and in no time at all Goldilocks fell fast asleep.

In a little while, the three bears came back from their walk in the forest. They saw at once that somebody had pushed open the door of their house and had been inside.

Father Bear looked around, then roared in a great big growly voice,

"SOMEBODY HAS BEEN SITTING IN MY CHAIR!"
Mother Bear said in a quiet gentle voice,

"Somebody has been sitting in my chair!"
Then Little Bear said in a small squeaky baby voice,

"Somebody has been sitting in my chair, and has broken it!"

Then Father Bear looked at his bowl of porridge and saw the spoon in it, and he said in his great big growly voice,

"SOMEBODY HAS BEEN EATING MY PORRIDGE!"

Then Mother Bear saw that her bowl had a spoon in it, and said in her quiet gentle voice,

"Somebody has been eating my porridge!"

Little Bear looked at his porridge bowl and said in his small squeaky baby voice,

"Somebody has been eating my porridge, and has eaten it all up!"

Then the three bears went upstairs, and Father Bear saw at once that his bed was untidy, and he said in his great big growly voice,

"SOMEBODY HAS BEEN SLEEPING IN MY BED!"

Mother Bear saw that her bed, too, had the bedclothes turned back, and she said in her quiet gentle voice,

"Somebody has been sleeping in my bed!"

Then Little Bear looked at his bed and said in his small squeaky baby voice,

"Somebody is sleeping in my bed, NOW!"

He squeaked so loudly that Goldilocks woke up with a start. She jumped out of bed, and away she ran, down the stairs and out into the forest. And the three bears never saw her again.

Cinderella

There was once a gentleman who lived in a fine house, with his pretty daughter. His kind and gentle wife had died, so the gentleman married again. His new wife was not at all kind or pretty. She had been married before and had two daughters who were known, behind their backs, as the Ugly Sisters.

Although they had no reason to be unkind, the two sisters were horrid to their new stepsister. They ordered her about, scolded her and made her do all the work in the big house. Her clothes became ragged and thin and far too small. "We've no money to spare for you," the two sisters would laugh. The poor girl was always cold and tired. In the evenings she would rest on a stool close to the fire, almost in the cinders and ashes.

"Cinderella. That's the perfect name for you," jeered the stepsisters when they saw her trying to keep warm. Cinderella had too sweet a nature to complain, and her father was much too busy to notice how badly his new wife and his stepdaughters treated her.

The king and queen of their country had a son who was not married, and they planned a big ball for this prince in the hope that he might find a bride. Invitations were sent to princesses in the neighboring countries and to all the big houses in their own country. When a large invitation card to the royal ball arrived at Cinderella's house, there was a great flurry of excitement. New dresses were chosen for the Ugly Sisters and their mother, and nobody talked about anything except the ball.

"I am sure the prince will fall in love with me," said one sister, smiling at herself in the mirror.

"You silly fool," said the other, pushing her aside. "He won't be able to resist falling in love with me. Just think, one day I could be the queen," and she pretended she was the queen already as she ordered Cinderella to get another pair of shoes for her to try on. No one thought of asking Cinderella if she would like to go to the ball. They scarcely even noticed her as they rushed around trying on different wigs, fans and gloves to go with their new ball dresses.

At last, the day of the ball came, and Cinderella worked harder than ever, helping the Ugly Sisters and her stepmother to get ready. They quarreled with each other all day, and by the time the carriage drove away to the king's palace, with all the family in it, Cinderella was glad to have some peace. But as she sat on her stool by the fire she could not help a tear falling onto the ashes for she wished that she could have gone with them.

Suddenly she blinked as she found she was not alone. A beautiful lady stood before her with a silver wand in her hand.

Cinderella gasped as the lady said,
"Cinderella, I am your fairy
godmother. Don't cry but tell me
what those tears are for?"

At her kind words, Cinderella
dried her eyes,
"I wish, oh how I wish, I could have gone to the ball too."

"So you shall," said her fairy godmother, "but first we have
some work to do."

"Oh no," sighed Cinderella, "not work, not more work."

"Yes, work!" said her godmother, "for if you are to go to the
ball, I cannot send you as you are. But we will do it together.
First, fetch me the largest pumpkin you can find in the garden."

Cinderella fetched the largest pumpkin she could see and in a
flash and wave of her wand, her fairy godmother had turned the
pumpkin into a gleaming golden coach.

"Now we need a few horses," said her godmother. "Look in
the mouse trap and see if there is anything there we can use."

Cinderella ran to the larder where there were six mice running
around in a cage. Once more Cinderella watched her godmother
wave her wand. There, suddenly, harnessed to the coach, were
six shining dappled horses, stamping their feet, impatient to be
off.

"Those horses need a coachman," decided the godmother.
"Look in the rat trap, Cinderella." There were three rats in the
trap and as the godmother touched the largest rat with her wand,
it disappeared. But now up in front of the coach sat a fine, plump,
whiskery coachman in smart uniform.

"Go and look behind the water barrel, Cinderella," said
her godmother, "and see if you can find something there we can
use for footmen."

Cinderella ran to the water barrel and brought to her godmother two lizards. At the wave of her wand they were trans-
formed into splendid footmen who jumped up on to the back of the
coach as if they had done this all their lives.

"There now, Cinderella, your coach is ready," said her godmother with a smile. "Soon you will be able to go to the ball."

"How can I go like this?" sighed Cinderella, looking down in despair at her ragged clothes and bare feet. But even as she hung her head, her godmother touched her with her wand and her rags turned into a shimmering gown. Cinderella gasped. On her feet she was wearing the prettiest pair of glass shoes she had ever seen.

As Cinderella stepped into the coach her godmother gave her a strict warning. "The magic will only last until midnight, and then everything will return to what it was before. Be sure you leave the ball before midnight, Cinderella."

When Cinderella's coach arrived at the palace the word went round that a beautiful lady had arrived in such a splendid coach that she must be a princess. The prince himself came down the steps to greet her. Stunned by her beauty he wanted to dance with her at once and led her straight to the ballroom. The other guests fell silent and the musicians stopped playing as everyone gazed in wonder at the lovely girl with the prince. Even the king sat up and remarked to the queen that it was a long time since he had seen such a pretty girl. The prince signaled to the musicians to play again and then took Cinderella in his arms and danced with her.

All evening the prince stayed at Cinderella's side. No one knew who she was. Not even the Ugly Sisters recognized her, even though Cinderella spoke to them and gave them some of the sweets the prince had given her. Cinderella herself was so happy she did not notice how quickly the time was flying by.

Suddenly she heard the clock strike the first stroke of midnight. With a small cry she escaped from the prince and ran towards the door of the palace. The prince lost sight of her although he followed as closely as he could. As the great clock continued to strike Cinderella ran down the steps, and into the courtyard. She did not even have time to pick up one of her shoes that came off as she ran.

The prince questioned everyone carefully but no one had seen the beautiful lady leave. The guards at the gate swore the only person who had gone through was a young raggedly-dressed girl. No one noticed the pumpkin in the corner of the courtyard or some mice, a rat and a pair of lizards that slunk into a dark corner. However the prince did find on the steps a glass shoe, and he recognized it as one of the elegant shoes the mysterious and lovely lady had worn.

The ball went on for many more hours so Cinderella reached home before her family, although she had to walk. The next day they could talk of nothing but the beautiful girl who had captured the prince's heart, of how she had disappeared so suddenly and how no one knew her name. The Ugly Sisters even boasted to Cinderella how lucky they had been to talk to the stranger and how kind she had been to them. Cinderella smiled as they talked but never said a word.

Later that week a proclamation was given from the palace that the prince was looking for the guest who had worn the glass shoe. His servants would tour the country with it until they found the lady whose foot it fitted and the prince would marry that lady. The prince, unable to think of anything except the lovely lady, traveled round with his servants but time and again he was disappointed as the shoe failed to fit any lady's foot.

At last they came to Cinderella's house. The Ugly Sisters were waiting.

"Let me try first," cried one, holding out her foot, and pushing as hard as she could to squeeze it into the shoe. But however hard she tried, she could not get the shoe on. At last she gave up and laughed at her sister's efforts as she, too, squeezed and pushed to get her foot into the tiny glass shoe. When she had failed, the palace servants asked if there were any more young ladies in the house, at which Cinderella stepped forward.

"You!" laughed and jeered the Ugly Sisters. "You were not even at the ball."

"The prince wants all young ladies to try," said one of the royal servants sternly.

Cinderella put her foot out and the glass shoe slipped on as though it had been made for her. Then there was a gasp of surprise as Cinderella drew from behind her back a second shoe which she put on her other foot. The prince came forward and held out his arms, and at the same moment the fairy godmother appeared and touched Cinderella with her wand. Instantly her ragged clothes changed into a beautiful dress, and everyone stared in amazement as Cinderella became the lovely stranger at the ball.

The prince asked Cinderella to marry him and Cinderella replied that there was nothing she would like more. The Ugly Sisters begged Cinderella to forgive them for their unkindness and she happily agreed. There was a fine royal wedding for Cinderella and the prince and some months later Cinderella found husbands at court for both the Ugly Sisters. Everyone agreed that Cinderella was as kind as she was beautiful. The prince loved her dearly and they all lived happily for a long, long time.

The Gingerbread Man

An old woman was baking one day, and she made some gingerbread. She had some dough left over, so she made the shape of a little man. She made eyes for him, a nose and a smiling

mouth all of currants, and placed more currants down his front to look like buttons. Then she laid him on a baking tray and put him in the oven.

After a little while, she heard something rattling at the oven door. She opened it and to her surprise out jumped the little gingerbread man she had made. She tried to catch him as he ran across the kitchen, but he slipped past her, calling as he ran:

"Run, run, as fast as you can,
You can't catch me, I'm the gingerbread man!"

She chased after him into the garden where her husband was digging. He put down his spade and tried to catch him too, but as the gingerbread man sped past him he called over his shoulder:

"Run, run, as fast as you can,

You can't catch me, I'm the gingerbread man!"

As he ran down the road he passed a cow. The cow called out, "Stop, gingerbread man! You look good to eat!" But the gingerbread man laughed and shouted over his shoulder:

"I've run from an old woman

And an old man.

Run, run, as fast as you can,

You can't catch me, I'm the gingerbread man!"

The cow ran after the old woman and the old man, and soon they all passed a horse. "Stop!" called out the horse, "I'd like to eat you." But the gingerbread man called out:

"I've run from an old woman

And an old man,

And a cow!

Run, run, as fast as you can,

You can't catch me, I'm the gingerbread man!"

He ran on, with the old woman and the old man and the cow and the horse following, and he went past a party of people haymaking. They all looked up as they saw the gingerbread man, and as he passed them he called out:

"I've run from an old woman,
And from an old man,
And a cow and a horse.
Run, run, as fast as you can,
You can't catch me, I'm the gingerbread man!"

The haymakers joined in the chase behind the old woman and the old man, the cow and the horse, and they all followed him as he ran through the fields. There he met a fox, so he called out to the fox:

"Run, run, as fast as you can,
You can't catch me, I'm the gingerbread man!"

But the sly fox said, "Why should I bother to catch you?" although he thought to himself, "That gingerbread man would be good to eat."

Just after he had run past the fox the gingerbread man had to stop because he came to a wide, deep, swift-flowing river. The fox saw the old woman and the old man, the cow, the horse and the haymakers all chasing the gingerbread man so he said,

"Jump on my back, and I'll take you across the river!"

The gingerbread man jumped on the fox's back and the fox began to swim. As they reached the middle of the river, where the water was deep, the fox said,

"Can you stand on my head, Gingerbread Man, or you will get wet?" So the gingerbread man pulled himself up and stood on the fox's head. As the current flowed more swiftly, the fox said,

"Can you move on to my nose, Gingerbread Man, so that I can carry you more safely? I would not like you to drown." The gingerbread man slid on to the fox's nose.
But when they reached the bank
on the far side of the river,
the fox suddenly went SNAP! The
gingerbread man disappeared
into the fox's mouth, and was
never seen or heard of again.

Three Billy Goats Gruff

Once upon a time there were three goats who all lived together. They were known as the Three Billy Goats Gruff. All of them had curly horns and tufted beards. They lived in a village where there was not always enough food for them, so they loved to cross over a wooden bridge to the other side of the valley to munch the rich grass in the meadows there.

A deep river ran under the bridge, and beside the river and under the bridge lived a fierce troll. He had a long nose, huge eyes and big teeth. He was an ugly, bad-tempered troll and, more than anything, he hated people or animals to cross the bridge. If he could catch them, he would eat them. The three billy goats had to try and get across to the valley without disturbing the troll, if they possibly could.

One day the troll was lying under the bridge when he heard the sound of steps TRIP TRAP, TRIP TRAP on the wooden planks above him.

"Who goes there?" roared the troll angrily.

The smallest Billy Goat Gruff was on the bridge, and he called out in a small frightened voice,

"It is only I, the little Billy Goat Gruff."

"Then I will eat you for my dinner," roared the troll.

"No, no," pleaded the little Billy Goat Gruff. "Let me cross over and eat the grass on the other side and I will grow fatter. My brother, the middle-sized Billy Goat Gruff, will be coming along soon. Why don't you wait and eat him?"

"Very well," grumbled the troll, and settled down under the bridge to wait for the middle-sized Billy Goat Gruff.

Before long, he heard TRIP TRAP, TRIP TRAP on the wooden planks above him.

"Who goes there?" roared the troll.

"It is I, the middle-sized Billy Goat Gruff," replied the goat in a middle-sized voice.

"Then I shall eat you for my dinner," roared the troll.

"I think," said the middle-sized Billy Goat Gruff, "you would do better to wait for my brother, the big Billy Goat Gruff. He will make a much better dinner, and meanwhile I shall be able to get fatter in those meadows over there."

"Very well," huffed the troll. He heard the middle-sized Billy Goat Gruff go TRIP TRAP, TRIP TRAP over the bridge and settled down to wait for the big Billy Goat Gruff.

Before long the big Billy Goat Gruff came along. The troll heard his hooves on the bridge above him. This time the TRIP TRAP, TRIP TRAP was loud and heavy.

"Who goes there?" roared the troll.

"It is I, the big Billy Goat Gruff," called the big goat in a big gruff voice and he sounded almost as fierce as the troll.

"Then I shall eat you for my dinner," bellowed the troll.

"Oh no you won't," replied the big goat, "for I have sharp horns and will kill you first."

The troll was so angry that he leapt out from underneath the bridge and attacked the big Billy Goat Gruff. But the big goat was waiting for him and stood firm, with his head down and his horns ready. The troll was tossed in the air and fell with a tremendous SPLASH far down into the deep river where he drowned.

The big Billy Goat Gruff went on his way to join his two brothers, TRIP TRAP, TRIP TRAP over the bridge and into the meadows. Now every morning and evening they could come and go over the bridge as they pleased, and I'm sorry to say that they all grew very fat indeed.

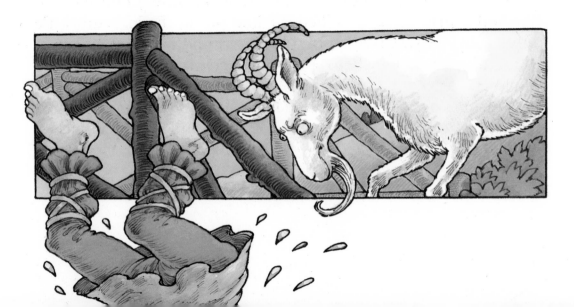

The Patchwork Quilt

Joan Aiken

Far in the north, where the snow falls for three hundred days each year, and all the trees are Christmas trees, there was an old lady making patchwork. Her name was Mrs Noot. She had many, many little three-cornered pieces of cloth – boxes full and baskets full, bags full and bundles full, all the colors of the rainbow. There were red pieces and blue pieces, pink pieces and golden pieces. Some had flowers on, some were plain.

Mrs Noot sewed twelve pieces into a star. Then she sewed the stars together to make bigger stars. And then she sewed *those* together. She sewed them with gold thread and silver thread and white thread and black thread.

What do you suppose she was making?

She was making a quilt for the bed of her little grandson Nils. She had nearly finished. When she had put in the last star, little Nils would have the biggest and brightest and warmest and most beautiful quilt in the whole of the north country – perhaps in the whole world.

While his granny sewed, little Nils sat beside her and watched the way her needle flashed in and out of the colored pieces, making little tiny stitches.

Sometimes he said,

"Is it nearly done, Granny?"

He had asked her this question every day for a year. Each time he asked it, Mrs Noot would sing,

> "Moon and candle
> Give me your light,
> Fire in the hearth
> Burn clear, burn bright.
>
> Needle fly swiftly,
> Thread run fast,
> Until the quilt
> Is done at last.
>
> The finest quilt
> That ever was,
> Made from more than
> A thousand stars!"

This was a magic song, to help her sew quickly. While she sang it, little Nils would sit silent on his stool, stroking the bright colors of the quilt. And the fire would stop crackling to listen, and the wind would hush its blowing.

Now the quilt was nearly done.

It would be ready in time for Nils's birthday.

Far, far to the south of Mrs Noot's cottage, in the hot, dry country where there is no grass and it rains only once every three years, a wizard lived in the desert. His name was Ali Beg.

Ali Beg was very lazy. All day he slept in the sun, lying on a magic carpet, while twelve camels stood around it, shading him. At night he went flying on his carpet. But even then the unhappy camels were not allowed to sit down. They had to stand in a square, each with a green lamp hanging on a chain round its neck, so that when Ali Beg came home he could see where to land in the dark.

The poor camels were tired out, and very hungry too, because they never had enough to eat.

As well as being unkind to his camels, Ali Beg was a thief. Everything he had was stolen – his clothes, his magic carpet, his camels, even the green lights on their necks. (They were really traffic lights; Ali Beg had stolen them from the city of Beirut one day as he flew over, so all the traffic had come to a stop.)

In a box, Ali Beg kept a magic eye which could see all the beautiful things everywhere in the world. Every night he looked into the eye and chose something new to steal.

One day, when Ali Beg was lying fast asleep, the eldest of the camels said, "Friends, I am faint with hunger. I must have something to eat."

The youngest camel said, "As there is no grass, let us eat the carpet."

So they began to nibble the edge of the carpet. It was thick and soft and silky. They nibbled and nibbled, they munched and munched, until there was nothing left but the bit under Ali Beg.

When he woke up he was very angry.

"Wicked camels! I am going to beat you with my umbrella and you shall have no food for a year. Now I have all the trouble of finding another carpet."

When he had beaten the camels, Ali Beg took his magic eye out of its box.

He said to it:

"Find me a carpet
Magic Eye,
To carry me far
And carry me high."

28

Then he looked into the magic eye to see what he could see. The eye went dark, and then it went bright.

What Ali Beg could see then was the kitchen of Mrs Noot's cottage. There she sat, by her big fireplace, sewing away at the wonderful patchwork quilt.

"Aha!" said Ali Beg. "I can see that is a magic quilt – just the thing for me."

He jumped on what was left of the magic carpet. He had to sit astride, the way you do on a horse, because there was so little left.

"Carry me, carpet,
Carry me fast,
Through burning sun,
Through wintry blast.

With never a slip
And never a tilt,
Carry me straight
To the magic quilt."

The piece of carpet carried him up into the air. But it was so small it could not go very fast. In fact, it went so slowly that, as it crept along, Ali Beg was burned black by the hot sun. Then, when he came to the cold north country where Mrs Noot lived, he was frozen by the cold.

By now night had fallen. The carpet was going slower and slower and slower – lower and lower and lower. At last it sank down on a mountain top. It was quite worn out. Ali Beg angrily stepped off and walked down the mountain to Mrs Noot's house.

He looked through the window.

Little Nils was in bed fast asleep. Tomorrow would be his birthday.

Mrs Noot had sat up late to finish the quilt. There was only one star left to put in.

But she had fallen asleep in her chair, with the needle halfway through a patch.

Ali Beg softly lifted the latch.

He tiptoed in.

Very, very gently, so as not to wake Mrs Noot, he pulled the beautiful red and blue and green and crimson and pink and gold quilt from under her hands. He never noticed the needle. Mrs Noot never woke up.

Ali Beg stole out of the door, carrying the quilt.

He spread it out on the snow. Even in the moonlight, its colors showed bright. Ali Beg sat down on it. He said,

"By hill and dale,
Over forest and foam
Carry me safely,
Carry me home!"

Old Mrs Noot had stitched a lot of magic into the quilt as she sewed and sang. It was even better than the carpet. It rose up into the air and carried Ali Beg south towards the hot country.

When Mrs Noot woke and found her beautiful quilt gone, she and little Nils hunted for it everywhere, but it was not in the kitchen – nor in the woodshed – nor in the forest – nowhere.

Although it was his birthday, little Nils cried all day.

Back in the desert, Ali Beg lay down on the quilt and went to sleep. The camels stood round, shading him.

Then the youngest camel said, "Friends, I have been thinking. Why should we keep the sun off this wicked man while he sleeps on a soft quilt? Let us roll him onto the sand and sit on the quilt ourselves. Then we can make it take us away and leave him behind."

Three camels took hold of Ali Beg's clothes with their teeth and pulled him off the quilt. Then they all sat on it in a ring, round the star-shaped hole in the middle. (Luckily it was a *very* big quilt.)

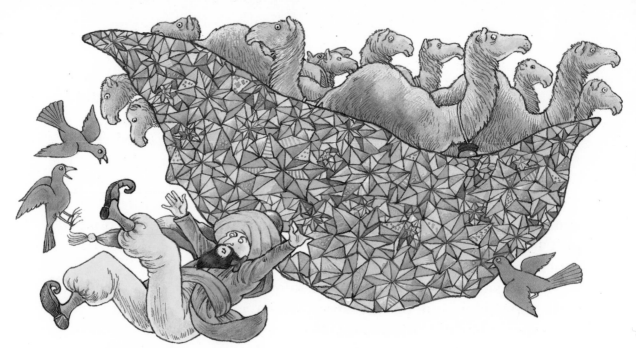

The eldest camel said,

"Beautiful quilt,
So fine and grand,
Carry us home
To your native land."

At once the quilt rose up in the air, with all the camels sitting on it.

At that moment, Ali Beg woke. He saw them up above him. With a shout of rage, he jumped up and made a grab for the quilt. His fingers just caught in the star-shaped hole.

The quilt sailed along with Ali Beg hanging underneath.

The youngest camel said, "Friends, let us get rid of Ali Beg. He is too heavy for this quilt."

So all the camels humped and bumped and thumped, they knocked and rocked, they slipped and tipped, they wriggled and jiggled, until the needle which Mrs Noot had left sticking through a patch ran into Ali Beg's finger. He gave a yell and let go. He fell down and down, down and down and down, until he hit the sea with a great SPLASH.

And that was the end of Ali Beg.

But the quilt sailed on, with the camels. As they flew over Beirut, they threw down the twelve green traffic lights.

When at last they landed outside Mrs Noot's house, Nils came running out.

"Oh, Granny!" he cried. "Come and see! The quilt has come back! And it has brought me twelve camels for a birthday present."

"Dear me," said Mrs Noot, "I shall have to make them jackets, or they will find it too cold in these parts."

So she made them beautiful patchwork jackets and gave them plenty of hot porridge to eat. The camels were very happy to have found such a kind home.

Mrs Noot sewed the last star into the patchwork and spread the quilt on Nils's bed.

"There," she said. "Now it's bedtime!"

Nils jumped into bed and lay proudly under his beautiful quilt. He went straight to sleep. And what wonderful dreams he had that night, and every night after, while his granny sat in front of the big fire, with six camels on either side of her.

The Great Big Turnip

Once upon a time, in Russia, an old man planted some turnip seeds. Each year he grew good turnips, but this year he was especially proud of one very big turnip. He left it in the ground longer than the others and watched with amazement and delight as it grew bigger and bigger. It grew so big that no one could remember ever having seen such a huge turnip before.

At last it stopped growing, and the old man decided that the time had come to pull it up. He took hold of the leaves of the great big turnip and pulled and pulled, but the turnip did not move.

So the old man called his wife to come and help him. The old woman pulled the old man, and the old man pulled the turnip. Together they pulled and pulled, but the turnip did not move.

So the old woman called her granddaughter to come and help. The granddaughter pulled the old woman, the old woman pulled the old man, and the old man pulled the turnip. Still the turnip did not move.

The granddaughter called to the dog to come and help. The dog pulled the granddaughter, the granddaughter pulled the old woman, the old woman pulled the old man, and the old man pulled the turnip. But the great big turnip stayed firmly in the ground.

The dog called to the cat to come and help pull up the turnip. The cat pulled the dog, the dog pulled the granddaughter, the granddaughter pulled the old woman, the old woman pulled the old man, and the old man pulled the turnip. They all pulled and pulled as hard as they could, but still the turnip did not move.

Then the cat called to a mouse to come and help pull up the great big turnip. The mouse pulled the cat, the cat pulled the dog, the dog pulled the granddaughter, the granddaughter pulled the old woman, the old woman pulled the old man, and he pulled the big turnip. Together they pulled and pulled and pulled as hard as they could.

Suddenly, the great big turnip came out of the ground, and everyone fell over.

Tim Rabbit
and
the Scissors

Alison Uttley

One day Tim Rabbit found a pair of scissors lying on the common. They had been dropped by somebody's mother, when she sat darning somebody's socks. Tim saw them shining in the grass, so he crept up very softly, just in case they might spring at him. Nearer and nearer he crept, but the scissors did not move, so he touched them with his whiskers, very gently, just in case they might bite him. He took a sniff at them, but nothing happened. Then he licked them, boldly, and, as the scissors were closed, he wasn't hurt. He admired the bright glitter of the steel, so he picked them up and carried them carefully home.

"Oh!" cried Mrs Rabbit, when he dragged them into the kitchen. "Oh! Whatever's that shiny thing? A snake? Put it down, Tim!"

"It's a something I've found in the grass!" said Tim, proudly. "It's quite tame."

Mrs Rabbit examined the scissors, twisting and turning them, until she found that they opened and shut. She wisely put them on the table.

"We'll wait till your father comes home," said she. "He's gone to a meeting about the lateness of the swallows this year, but he said he wouldn't be long."

"What have we here?" exclaimed Mr Rabbit when he returned.

"It's something Tim found," said Mrs Rabbit, looking proudly at her son, and Tim held up his head and put his paws behind his back, just as his father did at a public meeting. Mr Rabbit opened the scissors and felt the sharp edges.

"Why! They're shears!" he cried, excitedly. "They will trim the cowslip banks and cut the hay ready for the haystacks, when we gather our provender in the fall."

"Wait a minute!" he continued, snipping and snapping in the air, "Wait a minute. I'll show you." He ran out, carrying the scissors under his arm. In a few moments he came back with a neat bundle of grass, tied in a little sheaf.

"We can eat this in the peace and safety of our own house, by our own fireside, instead of sitting in the cold open fields," said he. "This is a wonderful thing you have found, Tim."

Tim smiled happily, and asked, "Will it cut other things, Father?"

"Yes, anything you like. Lettuces, lavender, dandelions, daisies, butter, and buttercups," answered Mr Rabbit, but he put the scissors safely out of reach on a high shelf before he had his supper.

The next day, when his parents had gone to visit a neighbor, young Tim climbed on a stool and lifted down the bright scissors. Then he began to cut 'anything'.

First he snipped his little sheep's-wool blanket into bits, and then he snapped the leafy tablecloth into shreds. Next he cut into strips the blue window curtains which his mother had embroidered with gossamer threads, and then he spoilt the tiny roller-towel which hung behind the door. He turned his attention on himself, and trimmed his whiskers till nothing was left. Finally he started to cut off his fur. How delightful it was to see it drop in a flood of soft brown on the kitchen floor! How silky it was!

He didn't know he had so much, and he clipped and clipped, twisting his neck and screwing round to the back, till the floor was covered with a furry fleece.

He felt so free and gay, so cool and happy, that he put the scissors away and danced lightly out of the room and on to the common like a dandelion-clock or a thistledown.

Mrs Rabbit met him as she returned with her basket full of lettuces and little cabbage-plants, given to her by the kind neighbor, who had a garden near the village. She nearly fainted when she saw the strange white dancing little figure.

"Oh! Oh! Oh!" she shrieked. "Whatever's this?"
Mother, it's me," laughed Tim, leaping round her like a newly-shorn lamb.

"No, it's not my Tim," she cried sadly. "My Tim is a fat fluffy little rabbit. You are a white rat, escaped from a menagerie. Go away."

"Mother, it *is* me!" persisted Tim. "It's Tim, your own Timothy Rabbit." He danced and leaped over the basket which Mrs Rabbit had dropped on the ground.

"No! No! Go away!" she exclaimed, running into her house and shutting the door.

Tim flopped on the doorstep. One big tear rolled down his cheek and splashed on the grass. Then another and another followed in a stream.

"It *is* me," he sobbed, with his nose against the crack of the door.

Inside the house Mrs Rabbit was gathering up the fur.

"It must have been Tim after all," she sighed. "This is his pretty hair. Oh, deary, deary me! Whatever shall I do?"

She opened the door. Tim popped his nose inside and sneezed.

"A-tishoo! A-tishoo! I'm so cold. A-tishoo! I won't do it again. I will be good," he sniffed.

"Come in, young rabbit," said Mrs Rabbit, severely. "Get into bed at once, while I make a dose of hot camomile tea."

But when Tim crept into bed there was no blanket. Poor Mrs Rabbit covered him with her own patchwork quilt, and then gave him the hot posset.

"Now you must stay here till your fur grows again," said Mrs Rabbit, and Tim lay underneath the red and blue patches of the bed-cover, thinking of the fun on the common, the leaping and galloping and turning somersaults of the little rabbits of the burrows, and he would not be there to join in.

Mr Rabbit was thoroughly shocked when he came home and saw his son, but he was a rabbit of ingenuity. He went out at once to borrow a spinning-wheel from an ancient rabbit who made coats to wrap Baby-Buntings in.

All day Mrs Rabbit wove the bits of fur, to make a little brown coat to keep Tim warm. When all the hairs were used up she pinned it round Tim with a couple of tiny sharp thorns from her pin-cushion.

"There you are, dressed again in your own fur," said she, and she put a stitch here and there to make it fit.

How all the animals laughed when Tim ran out on the common, with his little white legs peeping out from the bottom of the funny short coat! How ashamed he was of his whiskerless face!

"Baa! Baa! White sheep! Have you any wool?" mocked his enemies the magpies, when he ran near the wall where they perched. But Tim's fur soon grew again, and then his troubles were over.

He hung his little coat on a gorse-bush for the chaffinches to take for their nest, and very glad they were to get it, too. As for the scissors, they are still lying on the high shelf, and you may see them if you peep down the rabbit hole on the edge of the common where Tim Rabbit lives.

The Frog Prince

There was once a beautiful princess who had long dark hair and brown eyes which shone when she smiled, which she often did for she was a very happy person. She lived in a large palace with everything she could possibly want. But her favorite plaything was a golden ball. She carried it everywhere, throwing it happily into the air and catching it again.

One day she wandered through the palace gardens to a quiet spot where there was an old well. She sat on the edge of the well, tossing the ball up and down and laughing with pleasure to see it flash in the sun. All at once the golden ball slipped through her fingers, and fell into the well with a splash.

"Oh, my lovely ball," the princess cried, and her laughter turned to tears. She knew the water was very deep and did not know how she could get her ball back.

As she wept, she heard a croaky voice nearby. "Good. A gardener must be close by," she thought. "It's funny that I didn't notice him."

The princess looked around. No gardener appeared. Then she heard the voice again. "It's coming from inside the well," she decided. As she peered into the water, out jumped a frog which sat down beside her.

"If I go to the bottom of the well and fetch your golden ball, will you promise to let me eat at your table, sleep in your bed and will you kiss me, if I want you to, Princess?" asked the frog.

The princess was so upset about losing her ball that she did not think it odd that a frog was talking to her. Instead she thought, "How ridiculous! A frog could never get into the dining hall in the palace or up to my bedroom. But it might be able to rescue my golden ball for me."

So aloud she said, "Yes, Frog, I promise to do those things if you will bring my ball back to me."

The frog disappeared into the water and returned a few moments later with the golden ball in its mouth.

"Oh, thank you," said the princess. Snatching the ball, she ran quickly back to the palace for it was nearly time for dinner. She was so pleased to have the golden ball back that she forgot all about her promises to the frog.

As the princess, the king, and all the court were eating their meal, a curious noise was heard outside the dining hall. When the door was opened, the frog jumped right inside past the servants. The princess looked at it in dismay, and the king said crossly,

"Is this one of your jokes, bringing a frog into the palace?"

"No, father," she replied. "It's not a joke. This frog has come in by itself, but I promised that it could."

"A promise made must always be kept, my daughter," said the king solemnly. "Don't ever forget that! What exactly did you promise?"

43

"Well, that it should eat at my table," said the princess, not mentioning the other promises. So the king told one of the servants to bring up another chair to the table and place a silken cushion on it for the frog. But the frog jumped onto the princess's lap and started to eat from her plate. The princess tried very hard not to think about how cold and damp it was. But really she found it very unpleasant sharing her food with the frog.

That evening as she was getting ready for bed she found the frog in her bedroom.

"Oh, Frog," she exclaimed, "I suppose now you have come to sleep in my bed. Very well, a promise made has to be kept, my father says. You may sleep on the end of my bed."

The frog, however, jumped on to her pillow and sat there, cold and damp, waiting for the princess to get into bed. Reluctantly she edged under the covers.

"Please kiss me," then croaked the frog.

Now the princess did not want to break her word, nor did she want to kiss the frog. "If I do it quickly, that should be all right," she decided. As her lips touched the frog's smooth skin, she felt it change. Suddenly there before her was a handsome young man.

"Thank you," he cried, "thank you for releasing me from the spell a wicked witch put on me. She turned me into a frog, and told me the spell would only be broken if a princess agreed to let me eat at her table, sleep in her bed and then kiss me. I am a prince from a neighboring country and I have waited a long, long time to find a princess who could break the spell."

"Let us go down and tell my father," said the princess.

The king was delighted when he heard the prince's story and invited him to stay for a few days. The prince had loved the princess from the moment he first saw her by the well. Before long the princess fell in love with the prince and agreed to be his bride.

They had a grand wedding and then they rode off together to their new home in the prince's country. They lived happily for many years and when the princess wished to tease her husband, she would laugh and call him her 'Frog Prince'.

The Hare and the Tortoise

In the forest there was a clearing where many animals gathered each evening after going to the river to drink. The tortoise was usually the last to arrive, and the other animals would laugh at him as he plodded into the clearing.

"Come on, Slowcoach," they would call out as he came through the grass towards them. The tortoise would blink at them with his beady eyes and continue slowly on his way until he reached the spot where he wanted to settle down.

The liveliest of all the animals there was the hare. He ran so fast that he was always the first to arrive. "Just look at me," he was boasting one evening, "I can run faster than any of you. My speed and cleverness will always win."

The tortoise ambled into the clearing, last as usual. But to everyone's surprise he did not go to his usual place. Instead he went slowly across to the hare.

"Since you run so fast, could you beat me in a race?" he asked.

"*I,* beat *you,* in a *race!*" exclaimed the hare, and he fell on the ground and held his sides he laughed so much. "Of course I would beat you. You name the distance, Tortoise, but don't make it too far for your short little legs," and he roared with laughter again.

Most of the other animals laughed too. It did seem a very comic idea. The fox who thought they would see some good sport said,

"Come on then, Tortoise, name the distance and the time and then we will all come to see fair play."

"Let us start tomorrow morning, at sunrise," suggested the tortoise. "We'll run from this clearing to the edge of the forest and return to this spot again along the bank of the river."

"Why, it will take you all day to go so far, Tortoise. Are you sure you want to go ahead with it?" asked the hare. He grinned all over his face at the thought of the easy victory he would have.

"I am sure," replied the tortoise. "The first one back to this clearing will be the winner."

"Agreed!" said the hare, as the tortoise settled down in some long grass to sleep for the night.

The next morning the clearing was full of animals who had come to see the start of the great race. Some ran along to the edge of the forest to make sure that both animals followed the proper route. Others chose good places to watch along the way. The hare and the tortoise stood side by side. As the sun rose, the fox called out,

"Ready, steady, go!"

The hare jumped up and was out of sight almost at once. The tortoise started off in the same direction. He plodded along picking up his feet slowly, then putting them down only a little in front of where they had been before.

"Come on, Tortoise," called his friends anxiously. But he did not lift up his foot to wave at them as the hare had done. He kept on moving slowly forwards.

In a few minutes the hare was a long way from the starting line so he slowed down. "It's going to take the tortoise all day," he thought, "so there is no need for me to hurry." He stopped to talk to friends and nibble juicy grass here and there along the path.

By the time he reached half way the sun was high in the sky and the day became very hot. The animals who were waiting there saw the hare turn back towards the clearing. They settled down for a long wait for the tortoise.

As he returned by the river, the hot sun and the grass he had eaten made the hare feel sleepy.

"There's no need to hurry," he told himself. "Here's a nice shady spot," and stretching himself comfortably, he lay down. With paws beneath his head, he murmured sleepily, "It won't matter if Tortoise passes me, I'm much faster than he is. I'll still get back first and win the race." He drifted off to sleep.

Meanwhile the tortoise went on slowly. He reached the edge of the forest quite soon after the hare, for he had not stopped to talk to friends or eat tempting fresh grass. Before long, smiling gently, he passed the hare sleeping in the shade.

The animals in the clearing waited all day for the hare to return, but he did not arrive. The sun was setting before they saw the tortoise plodding towards them.

"Where is the hare?" they called out. The tortoise did not waste his breath in answering but came steadily towards them.

"Hurrah, Tortoise has won. Well done, Slowcoach!" the animals cheered. Only when he knew he had won the race did Tortoise speak,

"Hare? Oh, he's asleep back there by the river."

There was a sudden flurry and at great speed the hare burst into the clearing. He had woken and, seeing how long the shadows were, realized he had slept for much longer than he intended. He had raced back to the clearing but he was too late.

Tortoise smiled and said, "Slow and steady wins the race."

49

The Emperor's New Clothes

There was once an Emperor who was very vain. He loved to wear expensive clothes and tried to look as splendid as possible all the time. In his palace he had many rooms full of wardrobes and chests of fine clothes, and he liked to admire himself in long mirrors every time he changed, which he did several times a day. Cloth merchants and tailors grew rich by supplying clothes to the Emperor, and many beautifully colored and finely-woven materials were imported from far away lands for the Emperor to choose from. Many people used to laugh at him for his vanity, but he was too proud to notice.

One day two swindlers, pretending to be cloth merchants, came to the Emperor's Palace and asked to see the Emperor. They told the servants they had come from a faraway land with cloth more beautiful than anything the Emperor had ever seen before. When the palace servants asked to see the cloth, they were told it was for the Emperor's eyes alone.

The Emperor was so excited when he heard about the visitors that he arranged to see them immediately. They bowed low before him, and said that they had come to offer him the finest material in the whole world. It was so fine, they told him, that it had the magical quality of being invisible to anyone who was a fool. The Emperor asked to see it at once, so the two scoundrels opened their big wooden trunk and pretended to take out first one roll of cloth and then another. The Emperor blinked for he could see no cloth at all, even though the men did look as if they were unrolling some.

"I cannot let them think I am a fool," he thought to himself, so he pretended he could see the material perfectly well.

"Look at the lovely colors!" said one scoundrel.

"And the fine gold thread!" said the other, as they held up the invisible cloth before the Emperor.

"Yes," said the Emperor, sounding as enthusiastic as he could. "The colors are beautiful and the design magnificent."

He called in his wife and the Chief Minister and some of the courtiers to admire the cloth, and he explained about its magic qualities. They too could see no cloth at all, but they did not want the Emperor to think they were fools, so one by one they all admired the cloth. The Emperor was slightly disappointed because he had always thought that his wife and the Chief Minister were very foolish. But when they admired the material and talked about it, even putting out their hands to touch it, he decided he must have been wrong about them all the time. If they could see it, he certainly wasn't going to announce that he could not.

"Would your Majesty like us to take your measurements so that a suit can be made for you from these fine materials?" the merchants asked. We will make it up ourselves, for we can trust nobody else to cut it and stitch it,"

The Emperor agreed to have a suit made and pro-mised to reward the merchants well with money and jewels.

The scoundrels were given a room in the palace for their work. One material was chosen for the jacket, another for the trousers. A special shirt with lace collar and cuffs was also to be made from the material in the merchants' chest. The Emperor was very particular about where he wanted the buttons and how tight the waist was to be, and the scoundrels fussed around him, making careful notes of all his wishes.

The next day the Emperor went to try on his new clothes. He took off all his clothes and allowed the merchants to dress him, although he could not see what they were putting on. Then he walked across to the long mirror. He turned round and round but he could see no clothes at all. He called his Chief Minister who was astonished to see the Emperor standing before him with no clothes on, but not wishing to appear a fool, he said,

"How magnificent Your Majesty looks. How splendid! "Why not wear this wonderful suit of new clothes at your birthday procession next week?"

"The Chief Minister is not such a fool after all!" thought the Emperor, and agreed that he would wear the clothes when he rode through the city at the head of the great procession.

Around the city the news spread that the Emperor would be wearing the finest clothes ever seen on his birthday, and the crowds gathered in the streets to see him. Everyone had also heard that only wise people would see the new clothes as, to fools,

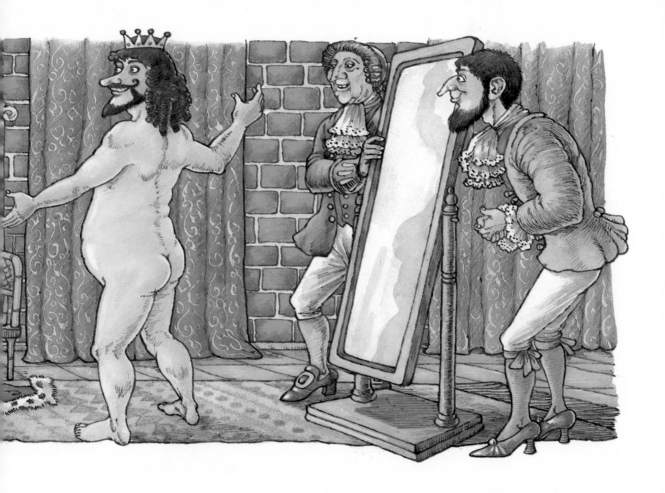

they would be invisible, and everyone had secretly decided that they would rather pretend to see them than let their friends and neighbors think they were fools.

The Emperor dressed with care on the day, flicking specks of dust off the wonderful new clothes he could not see, and admiring himself in the mirror for even longer than usual until the Master of Ceremonies came to say that the crowds were growing impatient. It was time for the procession to begin.

As he rode through the streets the Emperor heard the crowds cheering, and thought, "How lucky I am to rule over so many wise people. It seems there are no fools in my country, for everyone can see my new clothes."

But there was one small boy who had climbed a tree to get a better view of the Emperor. He had not heard that the Emperor's clothes were only visible to wise people, and he shouted out at once, "What has happened to his clothes? The Emperor hasn't anything on at all!"

The people around the boy laughed uneasily at him, then someone else shouted out, "The boy is right! The Emperor has got no clothes on!"

The laughter of the crowds turned on the Emperor and then on themselves, for they realized they had all been fools to believe the story of the magic clothes.

The Emperor was very angry with the scoundrels who had tricked him, and sent for them as soon as he got back to the palace. But they had fled, taking with them all the money and jewels the Emperor had given them. And you may be sure they were never seen in that country again.

Then the Emperor sent for the little boy who had climbed the tree and called out that he could not see the clothes. He told the boy he was the only wise person in the whole country, for he was not afraid to speak the truth. The Emperor promised him that he would be the Chief Minister when he grew up.

The Story of Persephone

This story is one of the tales that the ancient Greeks told about their gods. It is the story of Persephone, the lovely daughter of Demeter, Goddess of the Harvest.

Demeter traveled round the world with Persephone, talking to the trees and plants that produce food. As she passed the plants and touched them, they grew and flourished, and their fruit ripened. On hot days as she walked through a field of corn, the husks would swell and the corn would turn golden as she passed by. Whenever she visited orchards and vineyards, the apples, peaches, pears and grapes would be sweet and ready to eat. Persephone, who loved to go with her mother, would dance with joy to see how lovely the flowers looked when Demeter passed by.

One day Persephone asked her mother if she could go and play with her friends on the mountainside, while her mother went about her work. Demeter agreed, but warned Persephone not to stray too far. Then she went to visit some valleys where the harvest was late. Persephone and her friends scrambled happily over the mountainside. They found many flowers growing in the mountain meadows, and began to pick them, making garlands and chains as they wandered. Further and further they went, calling out to each other when they found a gentian, a lily or a mountain rose, until they were a long way from the valley where they had started.

Soon the meadows were shimmering in the hot mid-day sun. Persephone dropped behind her friends and sat on the grass to rest and to finish the garland she was making.

Suddenly there was a roar and a rushing sound. The side of the mountain seemed to split open and out galloped six great black horses, pulling a gleaming black chariot. Persephone was terrified and called out, "Mother, mother, help me!" But even as she called, the man driving the chariot leaned out and swept Persephone up into the chariot. He pulled at the reins to turn the horses and they galloped back into the mountain. With another roar and a crash the gap closed again leaving no sign of what had happened in the stony rock face by the green meadow.

Persephone's friends soon missed her and came back to look for her. They hunted everywhere and called and called, but there was no sign of her anywhere. At last they went back to tell Demeter. The goddess had been far away when Persephone had called for help but the wind had brought a faint cry to her ears, so she was already alarmed when she met the other children.

Together they searched up and down the mountain for hours, but could find no trace of Persephone until, in the evening, they came upon a fading garland of flowers lying in the grass. Now Demeter knew that something dreadful had happened to her daughter.

Something terrible had happened indeed. Persephone had been snatched by Hades, God of the Underworld. In his great black chariot, he drove her back to his palace of dark caverns deep inside the earth. The palace was full of beautiful things but Persephone found that she was very unhappy there. She missed the sunlight and the flowers, and all the colors of the world she had known, and most of all she longed to see her mother. She was so unhappy that she refused to eat in her new home. She just sat in a corner, pining for her old life. Hades did his best to please her. He loved her for her beauty and hoped to marry her, but Persephone time and again refused, saying that she wished only to return to the world above and her mother.

Meanwhile, Demeter continued to look for her daughter from one end of the world to the other. While she searched, she gave no thought at all to the harvest. Everywhere the crops failed and the farmers watched in despair as their corn did not ripen and their fruit withered on the trees.

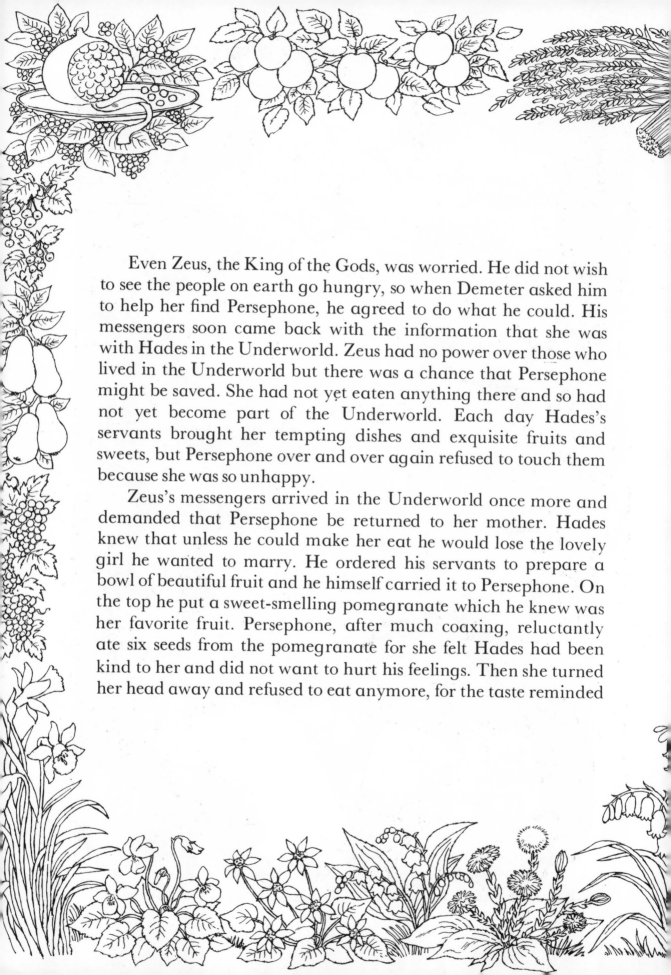

Even Zeus, the King of the Gods, was worried. He did not wish to see the people on earth go hungry, so when Demeter asked him to help her find Persephone, he agreed to do what he could. His messengers soon came back with the information that she was with Hades in the Underworld. Zeus had no power over those who lived in the Underworld but there was a chance that Persephone might be saved. She had not yet eaten anything there and so had not yet become part of the Underworld. Each day Hades's servants brought her tempting dishes and exquisite fruits and sweets, but Persephone over and over again refused to touch them because she was so unhappy.

Zeus's messengers arrived in the Underworld once more and demanded that Persephone be returned to her mother. Hades knew that unless he could make her eat he would lose the lovely girl he wanted to marry. He ordered his servants to prepare a bowl of beautiful fruit and he himself carried it to Persephone. On the top he put a sweet-smelling pomegranate which he knew was her favorite fruit. Persephone, after much coaxing, reluctantly ate six seeds from the pomegranate for she felt Hades had been kind to her and did not want to hurt his feelings. Then she turned her head away and refused to eat anymore, for the taste reminded

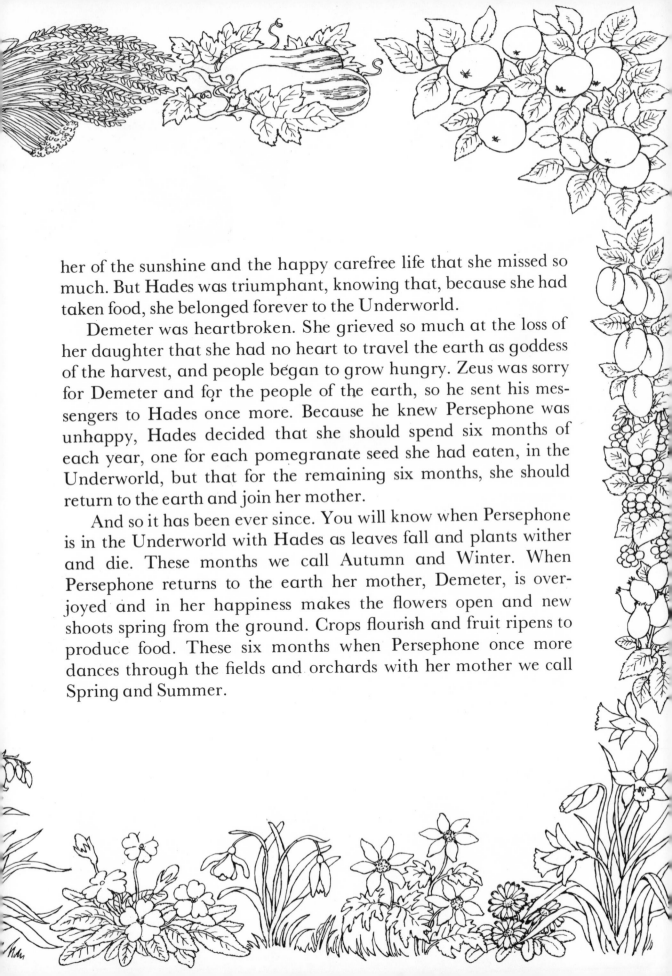

her of the sunshine and the happy carefree life that she missed so much. But Hades was triumphant, knowing that, because she had taken food, she belonged forever to the Underworld.

Demeter was heartbroken. She grieved so much at the loss of her daughter that she had no heart to travel the earth as goddess of the harvest, and people began to grow hungry. Zeus was sorry for Demeter and for the people of the earth, so he sent his messengers to Hades once more. Because he knew Persephone was unhappy, Hades decided that she should spend six months of each year, one for each pomegranate seed she had eaten, in the Underworld, but that for the remaining six months, she should return to the earth and join her mother.

And so it has been ever since. You will know when Persephone is in the Underworld with Hades as leaves fall and plants wither and die. These months we call Autumn and Winter. When Persephone returns to the earth her mother, Demeter, is overjoyed and in her happiness makes the flowers open and new shoots spring from the ground. Crops flourish and fruit ripens to produce food. These six months when Persephone once more dances through the fields and orchards with her mother we call Spring and Summer.

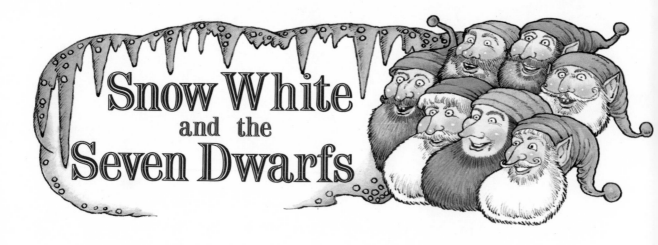

Snow White and the Seven Dwarfs

One winter's day, when the snow was falling, a beautiful queen sat sewing by a window. As she looked out on to the white garden she saw a black raven, and while she looked at it she accidentally pricked her finger with the needle. When she saw the drop of blood she thought to herself, "How wonderful it would be if I could have a little girl whose skin was as white as the snow out there, her hair as black as the raven and her lips as red as that drop of blood."

Not long afterwards the queen had a baby daughter, and when she saw her jet black hair, snowy white skin and red red lips she remembered her wish and called her Snow White.

Snow White grew up to be a pretty child, but sadly, after a few years, her mother died and her father married again. The new queen, Snow White's stepmother, was a beautiful woman too, but she was very vain. More than anything else she wanted to be certain that she was the most beautiful woman in the world. She had a magic mirror, and she used to look at herself in it each day and say:

"Mirror, mirror on the wall
Who is the fairest one of all?"
and the mirror would always reply,
"You, oh Queen, are the fairest one of all."
The queen would smile when she heard this for she knew the mirror never failed to speak the truth.

The years passed. Each year Snow White grew prettier and prettier, until one day, her stepmother looked in the magic mirror and said,

"Mirror, mirror, on the wall
Who is the fairest one of all?"
and the mirror replied,
"You, oh Queen, are fair, 'tis true,
But Snow White is fairer now than you."
The queen was angry and jealous. In a terrible rage she decided that Snow White should be killed.

She called for a hunter and told him to take Snow White far into the forest and to kill her there. In order to prove that Snow White was indeed dead, she commanded him to cut out Snow White's heart and bring it back to her. The hunter was very sad. Like everyone in the king's household he loved Snow White, but he knew he must obey his orders. He took her deep into the forest and, as he drew his knife, Snow White fell to her knees.

"Please spare my life," she begged. "Leave me here. I'll never return to the palace, I promise."
The hunter agreed gladly. He was sure the queen would never know he had disobeyed her. He killed a young deer and cut out its heart and took this to the queen, pretending it was Snow White's heart.

Poor Snow White was tired, lonely and hungry in the forest. She wandered through the trees, hoping she would find enough berries and nuts to keep herself alive. Then she came to a clearing and found a little house. She thought it must be a woodman's cottage where she might be able to stay, so she knocked at the door. When there was no answer, she opened it and went inside.

There she saw a room all spick and span with a long table laid with seven places – seven knives and forks, seven wooden plates and drinking cups, and on the plates and in the cups were food and drink. Snow White was so hungry she could not bear to leave the food untouched so she took a little from each plate and each cup. She did not want to empty one person's plate and cup only.

Beyond the table were seven little beds all neatly made. She tried out some of them, and when she found one that was comfortable, she fell into a deep sleep, for she was exhausted by her long journey through the forest.

The cottage was the home of seven dwarfs. All day long they worked in a nearby mine digging diamonds from deep inside the mountain. When they returned home that evening, they were amazed to see that someone had been into their cottage and had taken some food and drink from each place at their table. They were also surprised to find their beds disturbed, until one dwarf called out that he had found a lovely girl asleep on his bed. The Seven Dwarfs gathered round her, holding their candles high, as they marveled at her beauty. But they decided to leave her sleeping for they were kind men.

The next morning Snow White awoke and met the dwarfs, and she told them her story. When she explained how she now had no home, the dwarfs immediately asked her whether she would like to stay with them.

"With all my heart, I'd love to do that," Snow White replied, happy that she now had a home, and she hoped she could be of help to these kind little people.

The dwarfs suspected that Snow White's stepmother, the wicked queen, had magic powers and they were worried that she would find out that Snow White had not been killed by the hunter. They warned Snow White that when she was alone all day she should be wary of strangers who might come to the cottage.

Back at the palace the queen welcomed the hunter when he returned with the deer's heart. She was happy that now she was once more the most beautiful woman in the world. As soon as she was alone, she looked in her magic mirror and said confidently,

"Mirror, mirror, on the wall
Who is the fairest one of all?"

To her horror, the mirror replied,

"You, oh Queen, are fair, 'tis true
But Snow White is fairer still than you."

The queen trembled with anger as she realized that the hunter had tricked her. She decided that she would now find Snow White and kill her herself.

The queen disguised herself as an old pedlar woman with a tray of ribbons and pretty things to sell and she set out into the forest. When she came to the dwarfs' cottage in the clearing, she knocked and smiled a wicked smile when she saw Snow White come to the door.

"Why, pretty maid," she said pleasantly, "Won't you buy some of the wares I have to sell? Would you like some ribbons or buttons, some buckles, a new lacing for your dress perhaps?"

Snow White looked eagerly at the tray.

The queen could see that she was tempted by the pretty lacing and so she asked if she could help to tie it on for her. Then she pulled the lacing so tight that Snow White could not breathe, and fell to the floor, as if she were dead. The queen hurried back to her palace, sure that this time Snow White was really dead.

When the dwarfs came home that evening, they found Snow White lying on the floor, deathly pale and still. Horrified, they gathered around her. Then one of them spotted that she had a new lacing on her dress, and that it was tied very tightly. Quickly they cut it. Immediately Snow White began to breathe again and color came back to her cheeks. All seven dwarfs heaved a tremendous sigh of relief as by now they loved her dearly. After this they begged Snow White to allow no strangers into the cottage while she was alone, and Snow White promised she would do as they said.

Once again in the palace the queen asked the mirror,
"Mirror, mirror, on the wall,
Who is the fairest one of all?"
And the mirror replied,
"You, oh Queen, are fair, 'tis true,
But Snow White is fairer still than you."
The queen was speechless with rage. She realized that once more her plans to kill Snow White had failed. She made up her mind to try again, and this time she was determined to succeed.

She chose an apple with one rosy-red side and one yellow side. Carefully she inserted poison into the red part of the apple. Then, disguised as a peasant woman, she set out once more into the forest.

When she knocked at the cottage door, the queen was quick to explain she had not come to sell anything. She guessed that Snow White would have been warned not to buy from anybody who came by. She simply chatted to Snow White and as Snow White became more at ease she offered her an apple as a present. Snow White was tempted as the rosy apple looked delicious. But she refused, saying she had been told not to accept anything from strangers.

"Let me show you how harmless it is," said the disguised queen. "I will take a bite, and if I come to no harm, you will see it is safe for you too."

She knew the yellow side was not poisoned and took a bite from there. Thinking it harmless, Snow White stretched out her hand for the apple and also took a bite, but from the rosy-red side.

At once Snow White was affected by the poison and fell down as though dead. That evening when the dwarfs returned they were quite unable to revive her. They turned her over to see if her dress had been laced too tightly. But they could find nothing different about her. They watched over her through the night, but when morning came she still lay without any sign of life, and they decided she must be dead. Weeping bitterly, they laid her in a coffin and placed a glass lid over the top so that all could admire her beauty, even though she was dead. Then they carried the coffin to the top of a hill where they took turns to stand guard over their beautiful Snow White.

The queen was delighted that day when she looked in her mirror and asked,

"Mirror, mirror, on the wall
Who is the fairest one of all?"

and the mirror replied,

"You, oh Queen, are the fairest one of all."

How cruelly she laughed when she heard those words.

Not long after this a prince came riding through the forest and came to the hill where Snow White lay in her glass-topped coffin. She looked so beautiful that he loved her at once and he asked the dwarfs if he might have the coffin and take it to his castle. The dwarfs would not allow him to do this, for they too loved Snow White. But they did agree to let the prince kiss her.

As the prince kissed Snow White gently, he moved her head. The piece of poisoned apple fell from her lips. She stirred and then she stretched a little. Slowly she came back to life. Snow White saw the handsome prince kneeling on the ground beside her, and fell in love with him straight away. The Seven Dwarfs were overjoyed to see her alive once more and in love with a prince, and they wished them a long and happy life together.

When the queen far away in the palace heard from the mirror,

"You, oh Queen, are fair, 'tis true,
But Snow White is fairer still than you."

she was furious that Snow White had escaped death once more. And now the king discovered what mischief she had been up to, and banished her from his land. No one ever saw her or her mirror again.

As for Snow White, she said farewell to her kind friends the dwarfs, and rode away on the back of the prince's horse. At his castle they were married and they both lived happily forever afterwards.

Pix Pax Pox

Ruth Ainsworth

Once upon a time there was a witch, who lived in a small house in the middle of a deep, dark wood.

She had a tall steeple hat, a pointed nose and a whiskery chin. She wore a long cloak with silver patterns on it, made of half-moons and stars and magical shapes.

She had a black cat and a broomstick and a cauldron. The cauldron was a heavy iron pot which stood on the fire all day and simmered and bubbled. She also had a thick book of spells, full of close writing. She read this book every day and learned how to make magic.

The witch was very happy, sitting with her cloak wrapped round her, reading her Spell Book and learning how to make magic. While she was happy reading, the cat was doing the cooking and the broomstick was busy doing the housework.

Sometimes, when she was tired of reading, the witch went for a ride through the air on her broomstick. The cat clung on behind. She clung on very tightly because she was afraid she might fall off and lose one of her nine lives. Then she would only have eight left.

The cat was very thin and scrawny because she had to work so hard. She never had time to curl up by the fire and snooze, or to climb trees, or to chase mice and birds. The witch was always wanting a drink of nettle tea which the cat made in the cauldron and doled out with a heavy ladle.

The cat had to gather the nettles which grew around the house, and then boil them up, stirring all the time. Sometimes the witch fancied a drink of tea in the middle of the night and the cat had to get up and heat the cauldron and make it.

The broomstick was in a bad way too. He had to sweep the floor and brush the hearth and dust the furniture. He also had to shake the witch's feather bed till the feathers flew.

He was always tired and his bristles began to fall out. He would soon be bald. Sometimes he cried salt tears when he swept the bristles off the floor, with the crumbs and bits of nettle stalk.

Neither the cat nor the broomstick had a minute to spare to work in the garden. The witch's favorite plants were nettles and thistles and sloes, so the garden was wild and tangly.

But one day, a naughty little boy called Tim went for a walk in the woods, instead of going to school with all the other children. He came to the little round house and the witch cast a spell on him. She made him toil all day in the untidy garden. The thistles scratched him and the nettles stung him and the sloes were so sour, they gave him a pain if he ate one.

He was always hungry as he could not bear nettle tea. It tasted simply disgusting.

When the witch's back was turned, Tim made friends with the black cat and the broomstick.

At night, Tim had no proper bed to sleep in. He lay on a sack in the corner. When he could not get to sleep, he lay awake and made plans to escape.

He said to his friends, the cat and the broomstick: "I can read easy words. Shall I try to find a spell in the witch's Spell Book so that we can turn her into something?"

"Oh yes," agreed the cat and the broomstick, "What a good idea. What shall we turn her into?"

They thought of several good things, such as a black slug or a hedgehog or a rusty nail. But in the end they decided to turn her into a little wooden doll. Tim looked up 'doll' in the Spell Book, which said:

Sprinkle well with pepper and poppy seed and say 'Pix, Pax, Pox', three times.

There were a few poppies in the wild garden and there was plenty of pepper in the cupboard as the witch liked pepper in her tea instead of sugar.

So they made a mixture of poppy seed and pepper and sprinkled it on the witch while she lay asleep, in her feather bed. They all said, 'Pix, Pax, Pox,' three times. The witch shriveled and shrank and in a twinkling she turned into a little wooden doll, with a tiny pointed hat and a tiny pointed nose and a tiny pointed chin. All the whiskers had gone. It was a good spell. It worked.

After making this magic, they were all very tired. Tim crept into the witch's soft, feather bed with the cat curled up in his arms. The broomstick stretched out beside the fire, and they had a lovely, long sleep.

The next day they felt rested. Tim held the little doll tightly in his hand, and the cat and he climbed on to the broomstick, which took off into the air.

They flew up, up, over the tree-tops and came down at Tim's front gate. The broomstick knocked on the door, rat-a-tat-tat. Tim's mother opened the door and said:

"Come in everybody. Tea is ready." She gave Tim a hug and a kiss.

The cat was fed on milk and fish and she soon grew sleek and fat. The broomstick led an easy life in a warm corner, and was given a new coat of paint. His bristles began to grow again and he soon looked as good as new.

Tim's little sister, Rosie, took a great fancy to the little wooden doll and carried her everywhere. She called her Witchy.

As for Tim, he went to school every single day, and he never once ran off into the wood.

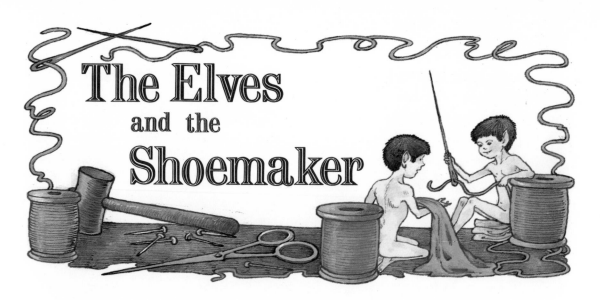

The Elves and the Shoemaker

Once upon a time there was a shoemaker who made very good shoes. But though he worked hard in his shop, times were difficult and he became poorer and poorer. One evening he cut out some shoes from his last bit of leather and laid the pieces out on his workbench to sew in the morning when the light was better. He put everything ready including the needles and thread.

"I may never make another pair of shoes," he sighed as he put the shutters over his shop window. "When I finish and sell this pair, I must buy food for my family. Then there will be nothing left over to buy leather to make more shoes."

The next morning when he went over to his workbench, the first thing he saw was a beautiful pair of shoes. He examined them carefully and realized they were made from the leather he had cut out the night before. The stitches were exquisite, very tiny and neat, and he knew the shoes were far better than any he could have made. Quickly he took down his shutters and placed this fine pair of shoes in his shop window.

The shoemaker was still puzzling over who could have made the shoes when the door opened and in came a grand gentleman. He asked to buy the shoes he had seen in the window and paid four times more than the shoemaker had ever asked before for a pair of shoes. With this money the shoemaker bought more leather and enough food to feed the family for several days.

That evening he sat at his workbench and cut out two pairs of shoes from his new leather. He left the pieces laid out as before, all ready to sew in the morning.

Then the shoemaker shut up the shop and went upstairs to join his family. In the morning he could scarcely believe his eyes, for there on his workbench were two beautiful pairs of shoes.

"Who could sew such tiny stitches?" he wondered, "and who could work so fast?"

He placed the shoes in the shop window. Rich people who had never visited his shop before came in to buy them, and paid a lot of money for them. The shoemaker took their money gladly, bought more leather and cut out more shoes.

Each night for many weeks the same thing happened. Two pairs, sometimes four pairs, were made in a night. The shoemaker became well-known for the excellent shoes he sold.

He cut out all sorts of shoes: men's shoes, ladies' shoes, party shoes, shoes with laces, shoes with straps, colored shoes, little children's shoes, dancing shoes. Each week he took even more money in his shop and his family were happy and well fed at last.

One night his wife suggested they should peep around the door of the workroom to see if they could find out who their night visitors were. As the town clock struck midnight, there was a scuffling and a scurrying by the window, and two little men squeezed through a crack in the shutters and hurried over to the workbench. They took tiny tools from their workbags and began to work. For several hours they stitched and hammered, and before dawn a row of new shoes lay on the workbench. The shoemaker and his wife rubbed their eyes in disbelief, wondering if they were dreaming, for the little men were scarcely bigger than the shoemaker's needles. Then, their work finished, the elves left everything neat and tidy and vanished the way they had come.

As it was just before Christmas, the shoemaker's wife suggested that the next evening they should put out presents for the little men who had helped them so much during the year. All the next day she was busy making two little green jackets and trousers with green woolen hats to match while her husband stitched two tiny pairs of boots.

74

The shoemaker and his wife laid these gifts out on the workbench that evening together with two little glasses of wine and plates with little cakes and cookies. They then kept watch again. They saw the elves scramble into the workshop and climb on to the workbench as they had done before. When they saw the little green jackets, trousers and hats and tiny boots the elves gave a shout of joy. Immediately they tried on the clothes and they were so delighted they danced around the workbench, waving their hats in the air. They sat down and ate all the food that had been left out and disappeared as before.

After Christmas the shoemaker still cut out shoes and left the pieces on his workbench but the elves never returned. They knew the shoemaker and his wife must have spied them for their clothes were the exact size, and fairy people do not like to be seen by humans.

The shoemaker did not mind however, for his shop was now so well-known that he had plenty of customers. If the shoemaker's stitches were not as tiny and neat as the elves' stitches no-one ever complained. Perhaps they never noticed. For many years he was known as the best shoemaker in town and he and his wife were never poor again. But they always remembered the elves and how they had been helped by them when times were hard.

Tales of Brer Rabbit

Uncle Remus was an old man who loved to tell stories about animals. Mostly he spun yarns about Brer Rabbit and Brer Fox and how more often than not Brer Rabbit got the better of Brer Fox.

One evening when the lady, whom Uncle Remus called Miss Sally, was looking for her little boy, she heard the sound of voices in the old man's cabin, and she saw the boy sitting by Uncle Remus. He was telling a story and this is how it began:

One hot summer day Brer Rabbit, Brer Fox, Brer Coon, Brer Bear and the other animals were clearing some ground so that it could be planted for the next year. The sun got hot and Brer Rabbit got tired. But he kept on working because he feared the others would call him lazy. Suddenly he hollered out that he had a thorn in his hand and he slipped off to find a cool place to rest. After a while he came across a well with two buckets hanging over it.

"That looks cool," says Brer Rabbit to himself, "I'll just get in there and take a nap," and with that, in he jumped. He was no sooner in one bucket than it began to drop down the well.

There has never been a more scared creature than Brer Rabbit at this moment. Almost straightaway he felt the bucket hit the water and there it sat. And Brer Rabbit, he kept as still as he could and just lay there and shook and shivered.

Now Brer Fox always had one eye on Brer Rabbit, and when he slipped off, Brer Fox sneaked after him and watched. He knew Brer Rabbit was up to something. Brer Fox saw Brer Rabbit come to the well, and he saw him jump in the bucket and then, lo and behold, he saw the bucket go down the well, out of sight.

Brer Fox was the most astonished fox that you ever laid eyes on. He sat there in the bushes and thought and thought but could not make head or tail of what was going on.

Then he said to himself, "Right down in that well is where Brer Rabbit keeps his money hidden. If that's not it, then he's discovered a gold mine. I'm going to see what's in there."

Brer Fox crept a little nearer, but he heard nothing. So he crept nearer again and still heard nothing. Then he got right up close and peered down into the well, but he could see nothing.

All this time Brer Rabbit was lying in the bucket scared out of his skin. If he moved the bucket might tip over and spill him out into the water. As he was saying his prayers, old Brer Fox hollered out,

"Heyo, Brer Rabbit, who are you visiting down there?"

"Who? Me? Oh, I'm just fishing, Brer Fox," says Brer Rabbit. "I just said to myself I'd sort of surprise you with a lot of fishes for dinner, so here I am, and here are all the fishes. I'm fishing for suckers, Brer Fox," says Brer Rabbit.

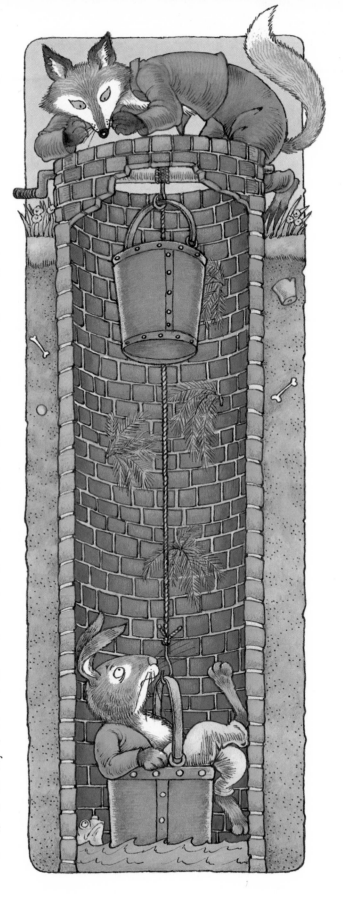

"Are there many down there, Brer Rabbit?" says Brer Fox.

"Lots of them, Brer Fox. Scores and scores of them. The water is alive with them. Come down and help me haul them in, Brer Fox," says Brer Rabbit.

"How am I going to get down, Brer Rabbit?"

"Jump into the bucket, Brer Fox. It will bring you down safe and sound."

Brer Rabbit sounded so happy that Brer Fox jumped into the other bucket and it began to fall. As he went down into the well, his weight pulled Brer Rabbit's bucket up. When they passed one another, half way up and half way down, Brer Rabbit called out,

"Goodbye Brer Fox, take care of your clothes,
For this is the way the world goes,
Some goes up and some goes down,
You'll get to the bottom all safe and sound."

Brer Rabbit's bucket reached the top of the well and he jumped out. He galloped off to the people who owned the well and told them that Brer Fox was down the well muddying their drinking water. Then he galloped back to the well and hollered down to Brer Fox,

"Here comes a man with a great big gun,
When he hauls you up, you jump and run."

"What then, Uncle Remus?" asked the little boy quickly, as the old man paused.

"My oh my," replied Uncle Remus, "in about half an hour both of them were back on the ground that was being cleared, working as though they'd never heard of any well, except every now and then Brer Rabbit burst out laughing. And old Brer Fox, he looked mighty sore."

The next evening the little boy had more questions,

"Didn't the Fox ever catch the Rabbit?," he asked Uncle Remus.

"He came mighty near it, honey, sure as you're born," replied Uncle Remus, "and this is how it happened."

One day Brer Fox got some tar and mixed it with some turpentine and fixed up a contraption which he called a Tar-Baby. He took this Tar-Baby and sat her in the road and then he lay in the bushes to see what was going to happen. He did not have to wait long because by and by along came Brer Rabbit all dressed up as fine as a jay-bird. Brer Rabbit pranced along *lippity-clippity, clippity-lippity* until he spied the Tar-Baby. He stopped in astonishment. The Tar-Baby just sat there and Brer Fox, he lay low.

"Morning!" says Brer Rabbit, "Nice weather this morning!" he says. But the Tar-Baby said nothing and Brer Fox, he lay low.

"Are you deaf?" says Brer Rabbit, "for if you are, I can holler louder."

The Tar-Baby stayed still and Brer Fox, he lay low.

"You're stuck up, that's what you are," shouts Brer Rabbit. "I'm going to teach you how to talk to respectable folks. If you don't take that hat off, I'll hit you."

But of course the Tar-Baby stayed still and Brer Fox, he lay low. Brer Rabbit drew back his fist and *blip*, he hit the side of the Tar-Baby's head. His fist stuck and he couldn't pull loose.

"If you don't let me loose I'll hit you again," says Brer Rabbit, and he swiped at the Tar-Baby with his other hand and that stuck too.

"Let me loose before I kick the stuffing out of you," hollers Brer Rabbit.

But the Tar-Baby said nothing. She just held on and Brer Rabbit soon found his feet stuck in the same way. Then he butted the Tar-Baby with his head and that stuck too.

Now Brer Fox sauntered out of the bushes, looking as innocent as a mocking-bird.

"Howdy, Brer Rabbit," he says, "you look sort of stuck up this morning," and he rolled on the ground with laughter. He laughed and laughed until he could laugh no more.

"And Brer Rabbit," Uncle Remus finished with a chuckle, "he was stuck as tight as tight could be."

The very next evening the little boy asked Uncle Remus sadly whether the Fox killed and ate the Rabbit when he caught him with the Tar-Baby.

"Now now, honey," said Uncle Remus, "don't you go crying over Brer Rabbit. You wait and see how he ends up." And he went on with the story.

'As Brer Rabbit struggled on the ground with the Tar-Baby, Brer Fox crowed triumphantly,

"Hah! I've got you this time and it's your own fault. No one asked you to strike up an acquaintance with the Tar-Baby. You just stuck yourself on to it, and now I'm going to make a fire and barbecue you."

Then Brer Rabbit began to talk in a very humble voice.

"I don't care," he says, "what you do with me as long as you don't throw me in that briar patch. Roast me, but don't throw me in the briar patch."

"It's so much trouble to kindle a fire, I think I'll hang you or drown you," says Brer Fox.

"Hang me as high as you please, drown me as deep as you please, Brer Fox, but don't fling me in that briar patch."

Now Brer Fox wanted to hurt Brer Rabbit as much as possible. So he picked him up by the hind legs and slung him right into the middle of the briar patch. He then waited to see what would happen next.

Suddenly he heard someone calling him. Way up the hill was Brer Rabbit sitting cross-legged on a log, combing tar out of his fur. Then Brer Fox knew he'd been tricked, and just to rub it in Brer Rabbit called out,

"Bred and born in a briar patch, Brer Fox, bred and born in a briar patch."

"With that he skipped off as lively as a cricket," said Uncle Remus, "and lived to trick old Brer Fox another day."

Little Red Riding Hood

There was once a pretty little girl who lived in a cottage on the edge of a wood. Her grandmother who lived at the other side of the wood had made her a warm red cape with a hood, and as she often wore it, she became known as Little Red Riding Hood.

One day her mother called her and said, "Little Red Riding Hood, will you take this basket of food to your grandmother as she isn't very well. Carry the basket carefully for I have filled it with some cakes, some fresh bread and some butter."

So Little Red Riding Hood put on her red cape and carrying the basket carefully she set off through the wood to her grandmother's house. As she went, she wandered off the path to pick some pretty flowers and to look at some butterflies. Then, quite unexpectedly, she met a wolf.

The wolf licked his lips when he saw the pretty little girl. But he could not risk eating her there as he could hear some woodmen working in a clearing close by.

"Where are you going, little girl?" he asked instead.

"I'm going to my grandmother," Little Red Riding Hood answered, "I have some presents for her as she is ill."

"And where does your grandmother live?" asked the wolf, thinking if he was clever he might be able to eat the little girl *and* her grandmother.

"Through the wood, and her's is the first cottage you can see," replied Little Red Riding Hood. She went on slowly through the wood, stopping here and there to add some more flowers to the bunch she was holding. The wolf watched her for a few minutes. Then he ran by the shortest route through the trees to the grandmother's cottage.

When he arrived there he knocked at the door.

"Who is there?" he heard an old lady call.

"It is me, Little Red Riding Hood, grandmother, with some presents for you," answered the wicked wolf, making his voice sound as much like Little Red Riding Hood's as he could.

"Pull the bobbin and the latch will go up," called the old lady from her bed.

The wolf pulled the bobbin, the latch went up, and he bounded into the room. In a trice he had gobbled up the poor old lady. He then put on her shawl and nightcap and got into her bed to wait for Little Red Riding Hood.

In a while there was a knock at the door.

"Who is there?" quavered the wolf, trying to make his voice sound as much like the old lady's as possible.

"It's me, Little Red Riding Hood," answered the girl. "I have brought you some food from my mother."

"Pull the bobbin and the latch will go up," called the wolf. The voice sounded rather gruff to Little Red Riding Hood.

She thought it must be because her grandmother had a sore throat. The wolf tugged the bedclothes up as far as he could under his chin as Little Red Riding Hood pulled the bobbin and walked into her grandmother's cottage.

In the bed she saw someone wearing a shawl and nightcap. She was rather puzzled. Her grandmother seemed quite different. So she said,

"What big eyes you have, grandmother!"

"All the better to see you with!" said the wolf.

"What big ears you have, grandmother!"

"All the better to hear you with!" said the wolf.

"What big teeth you have, grandmother!"

"All the better to eat you with!" said the wolf and he sprang out of bed. He pounced on Little Red Riding Hood about to gobble her up.

Little Red Riding Hood screamed with fright. Luckily the woodcutters had just come out of the wood and were passing the cottage. They rushed inside and killed the wolf instantly. One of them then cut him open and out jumped the grandmother, who was feeling rather shaken by her adventure. However, she was delighted to see Little Red Riding Hood, who gave her the food she had bought in her basket and the bunch of flowers.

Little Red Riding Hood took care never to talk to wolves again, and she always stayed on the path whenever she went through the wood to visit her grandmother.

The Ugly Duckling

One summer, when the corn was golden yellow and the hay was being dried in the fields, a mother duck was sitting on her nest of eggs. She sat in the rushes of a deep moat that surrounded a lovely country house and waited for her eggs to hatch. It was taking a very long time and she was getting very tired.

At last one day she felt a movement beneath her. The eggs began to crack and out popped tiny fluffy ducklings. All the eggs hatched except for one, which was larger than the rest. The mother duck was impatient to take her new ducklings swimming but could not leave the last egg unhatched. She sat for a few more days, and just as she was about to give up, she heard a tapping and out of the shell tumbled the oddest ugliest duckling she had ever seen.

She took the babies into the water and proudly watched as they all swam straightaway, even the ugly duckling. She led them in a procession around the moat, showing them off to the other ducks. As they bobbed along behind her she heard many quacks of admiration and praise for her fine family. But she also heard laughter and scorn poured on the ugly duckling at the end of the line.

"He has been too long in the egg," she explained, "he has not come out quite the right shape. But he is strong and will grow into a fine duck soon."

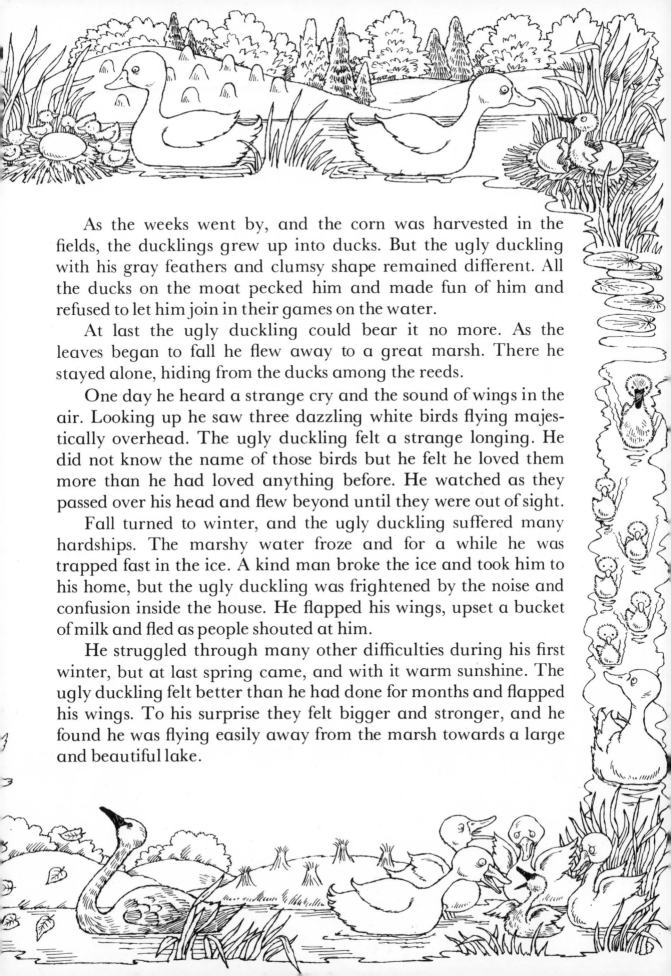

As the weeks went by, and the corn was harvested in the fields, the ducklings grew up into ducks. But the ugly duckling with his gray feathers and clumsy shape remained different. All the ducks on the moat pecked him and made fun of him and refused to let him join in their games on the water.

At last the ugly duckling could bear it no more. As the leaves began to fall he flew away to a great marsh. There he stayed alone, hiding from the ducks among the reeds.

One day he heard a strange cry and the sound of wings in the air. Looking up he saw three dazzling white birds flying majestically overhead. The ugly duckling felt a strange longing. He did not know the name of those birds but he felt he loved them more than he had loved anything before. He watched as they passed over his head and flew beyond until they were out of sight.

Fall turned to winter, and the ugly duckling suffered many hardships. The marshy water froze and for a while he was trapped fast in the ice. A kind man broke the ice and took him to his home, but the ugly duckling was frightened by the noise and confusion inside the house. He flapped his wings, upset a bucket of milk and fled as people shouted at him.

He struggled through many other difficulties during his first winter, but at last spring came, and with it warm sunshine. The ugly duckling felt better than he had done for months and flapped his wings. To his surprise they felt bigger and stronger, and he found he was flying easily away from the marsh towards a large and beautiful lake.

He alighted on the water and saw before him the three wonderful birds he had seen flying overhead several months before. As the swans glided smoothly over the lake, the ugly duckling felt drawn to them, but he was sure they would peck and tease him like the ducks because he was so ugly.

At last he thought, "It's better to be hurt or even killed by birds as lovely as these than to be teased by those ducks," and he floated slowly towards them. "Kill me, kill me," he whispered as he drew nearer and he bent his neck in shame.

All at once he saw a reflection in the smooth lake waters. A beautiful swan with glossy white feathers and a fine yellow beak stared up at him. He moved; the swan moved. He opened his wings; so did the swan. The ugly duckling suddenly realized – he was a swan.

The other swans swam gracefully towards him, welcoming him and stroking him with their beaks. Some children came running down to the lake and called out to their father.

"Look a new swan has appeared. He is more beautiful than any of the others!" and they threw pieces of bread into the water for him.

The young and beautiful swan felt quite shy with all this attention, and hid his head under his wing. But, as the lilac trees bent their branches down to the water and the sun shone warm and bright, he felt a deep happiness. He rustled his feathers, arched his sleek long neck and said to himself, "I never dreamed of such great happiness when I was the Ugly Duckling."

Nail Soup

One dark and stormy night, a tramp knocked on the door of a cottage and asked for shelter. An old woman answered the door and told the tramp sourly that he could come in if he wanted, but he must not expect any food for she had none in the house.

"And don't think you'll get a bed to sleep on either," she added, "as I only have one and that is where I sleep. You'll have to sleep on a chair."

The tramp was hungry, but he could see he wasn't going to get any food, so he sat by the fire and took an old nail out of his pocket and tossed it from hand to hand.

"Do you see this nail here?" he said at last. "You'd never believe it, but last night I made the finest soup I have ever eaten by cooking this nail, and what is more I still have it to make some more tonight. Would you like me to make you some nail soup?"

"Nail soup!" snorted the old woman. "I have never heard of such a thing. Don't talk nonsense." But the tramp could see she was curious.

"All I did," he told her, "was to boil it up in an old saucepan, and it was delicious."

"Well, since we have nothing else to do, and I have no food in the house, perhaps you would be good enough to show me how you do it," she said after a few minutes.

"You haven't a large pot and some water, have you?" asked the tramp.

"Why yes," said the old woman, handing a big cooking pot to the tramp and showing him where the water was. She watched as the tramp carefully filled the pot half full with water, placed it on the stove, and dropped in the nail. Then he sat down to wait.

From time to time, the old woman peeped into the pot to see how the soup was doing, and once when she lifted the lid the tramp said,

"Last night all that was needed was a little salt and pepper. I don't suppose you have any in the house?"

"I might have," said the old woman ungraciously, and from a cupboard she took salt and pepper which she dropped into the water with the nail.

The next time she lifted the lid, the tramp sighed, "What a pity you haven't got half an onion for that would make the soup even better than it was last night."

"I think I might just have an onion," said the old woman, quite excited by now at the thought of the nail soup, and she went to the larder to fetch an onion. As she opened the door, the tramp caught a glimpse of shelves stacked with food, but he said nothing until the onion had been in the pot for about ten minutes.

Then, stirring the soup again, he murmured to himself, "How sad that this fine onion has no carrots and potatoes to go with it." Just as he had hoped, the old woman quickly fetched some carrots and potatoes from the larder, peeled and chopped them, and put them in the pot.

By now, the soup was beginning to smell good, and it was not long before the tramp said that on nights when he could add a little meat to his nail soup, it was fit even for kings and queens. In a flash, the old woman had fetched some meat and put it in the pot.

While the soup was bubbling, the tramp looked around at the table. "It's a funny thing," he remarked, "but my nail soup always tastes better when I eat it at a table that is laid with pretty china and when there is a candle or two on the table."

The old woman, not to be outdone, put out her best tablecloth and got the best china off the dresser. Soon the table looked ready for a feast.

"What a shame," said the tramp, "that we have no bread to eat with this nail soup, but I remember you telling me there is no food in the house."

"I'll just look in the bread crock," said the old woman, and she pulled out a loaf that looked as though it had been baked that morning.

The soup now smelled quite delicious, and the tramp was longing to eat it, but he waited a few more minutes before saying,

"I am sorry there is no wine to drink with our nail soup, as I would have liked you to enjoy it with a glass of wine."

"Just a minute," said the old woman, and she fetched a fine-looking bottle of wine from the back of a cupboard and put it on the table with two glasses.

"Now the soup is ready. I hope you enjoy it," said the tramp heartily, and he fished the nail out with a spoon and put it in his pocket before carrying the soup over to the table.

They both had a wonderful meal. After the soup, which the old woman agreed was the best she'd ever tasted, she found some cheese and other good things in the larder. They told each other many stories, laughed a lot and had a very pleasant evening indeed.

As the candles burnt low, the old woman told the tramp to go and sleep in her bed, saying that she would be quite comfortable in a chair by the fire, and so the tramp went to bed and slept soundly.

As he left the next morning, he thanked the old woman for her kindness, but she said,

"No, no, I must thank you for showing me how to make soup from an old nail."

"It's what you add that makes the difference!" said the tramp, smiling as he walked away down the road, and he patted the nail in his pocket to make sure it was there for the next evening.

The Three Little Pigs

Once upon a time there were three little pigs. One day they set out from the farm where they had been born. They were going out into the world to start new lives and enjoy any adventures that might come their way.

The first little pig met a man carrying some straw, and he asked him if he might have some to build himself a house.

"Of course, little pig," said the man. He gave the little pig a big bundle of straw, and the little pig built himself a lovely house of golden straw.

A big bad wolf lived nearby. He came along and saw the new house and, feeling rather hungry and thinking he would like to eat a little pig for supper, he called out,

"Little pig, little pig, let me come in."
To which the little pig replied,
"No, no, by the hair of my chinny chin chin,
I'll not let you in!"
So the wolf shouted very crossly,
"Then I'll huff and I'll puff,
Till I blow your house in!"
And he huffed and he puffed, and he HUFFED and he PUFFED until the house of straw fell in, and the wolf ate the little pig for his supper that evening.

The second little pig was walking along the road when he met a man with a load of wood. "Please Sir," he said, "can you let me have some of that wood so that I can build a house?"

"Of course," said the man, and he gave him a big pile of wood. In no time at all, the little pig had built himself a lovely house. The next evening, along came the same wolf. When he saw another little pig, this time in a wooden house, he called out,

"Little pig, little pig, let me come in."

To which the pig replied,

"No, no, by the hair of my chinny chin chin,

I'll not let you in!"

So the wolf shouted,

"Then I'll huff and I'll puff,

Till I blow your house in!"

And he huffed and he puffed and he HUFFED and he PUFFED until the house fell in and the wolf gobbled up the little pig for his supper.

The third little pig met a man with a cartload of bricks. "Please Sir, can I have some bricks to build myself a house?" he asked, and when the man had given him some, he built himself a lovely house with the bricks.

The big bad wolf came along, and licked his lips as he thought about the third little pig. He called out,

"Little pig, little pig, let me come in!"

And the little pig called back,

"No, no, by the hair of my chinny chin chin,
I'll not let you in!"

So the wolf shouted,

"Then I'll huff and I'll puff,
Till I blow your house in!"

And the wolf huffed and he puffed, and he HUFFED and he PUFFED, and he HUFFED again and PUFFED again, but still the house, which had been so well built with bricks, did not blow in.

The wolf went away to think how he could trick the little pig, and he came back and called through the window of the brick house, "Little pig, there are some marvelous turnips in the farmer's field. Shall we go there tomorrow morning at six o'clock and get some?"

The little pig thought this was a very good idea, as he was very fond of turnips, but he went at five o'clock, not six o'clock, and collected all the turnips he needed before the wolf arrived.

The wolf was furious, but he thought he would try another trick. He told the little pig about the apples in the farmer's orchard, and suggested they both went to get some at five o'clock the next morning. The little pig agreed, and went as before, an hour earlier. But this time the wolf came early too, and arrived while the little pig was still in the apple tree. The little pig pretended to be pleased to see him and threw an apple down to the wolf. While the wolf was picking it up, the little pig jumped down the tree and got into a barrel. He rolled quickly down the hill inside this barrel to his house of bricks and rushed in and bolted the door.

The wolf was very angry that the little pig had got the better of him again, and chased him in the barrel back to his house. When he got there he climbed on to the roof, intending to come down the chimney and catch the little pig that way. The little pig was waiting for him, however, with a large cauldron of boiling water on the fire. The wolf came down the chimney and fell into the cauldron with a big SPLASH, and the little pig quickly put the lid on it.

The wicked wolf was never seen again, and the little pig lived happily in his brick house for many many years.

The Elephant and the Bad Baby

Elfrida Vipont

Once upon a time there was an Elephant. And one day the Elephant went for a walk and he met a Bad Baby. And the Elephant said to the Bad Baby, "Would you like a ride?" And the Bad Baby said, "Yes."

So the Elephant stretched out his trunk, and picked up the Bad Baby and put him on his back, and they went rumpeta, rumpeta, rumpeta, all down the road.

Very soon they met an ice-cream man. And the Elephant said to the Bad Baby, "Would you like an ice-cream?" And the Bad Baby said, "Yes."

So the Elephant stretched out his trunk and took an ice-cream for himself and an ice-cream for the Bad Baby, and they went rumpeta, rumpeta, rumpeta, all down the road, with the ice-cream man running after.

Next they came to a pork butcher's shop. And the Elephant said to the Bad Baby, "Would you like a pie?" And the Bad Baby said, "Yes."

So the Elephant stretched out his trunk and took a pie for himself and a pie for the Bad Baby, and they went rumpeta, rumpeta, rumpeta, all down the road, with the ice-cream man and the pork butcher both running after.

Next they came to a baker's shop. And the Elephant said to the Bad Baby, "Would you like a bun?" And the Bad Baby said, "Yes."

So the Elephant stretched out his trunk and took a bun for himself and a bun for the Bad Baby, and they went rumpeta, rumpeta, rumpeta, all down the road, with the ice-cream man, and the pork butcher, and the baker all running after.

Next they came to a snack shop. And the Elephant said to the Bad Baby, "Would you like some potato chips?" And the Bad Baby said, "Yes."

So the Elephant stretched out his trunk and took some potato chips for himself and some potato chips for the Bad Baby, and they went rumpeta, rumpeta, rumpeta, all down the road, with the ice-cream man, and the pork butcher, and the baker, and the snack shop man all running after.

Next they came to a grocer's store. And the Elephant said to the Bad Baby, "Would you like a chocolate cookie?" And the Bad Baby said, "Yes."

So the Elephant stretched out his trunk and took a chocolate cookie for himself and a chocolate cookie for the Bad Baby, and they went rumpeta, rumpeta, rumpeta, all down the road, with the ice-cream man, and the pork butcher, and the baker, and the snack shop man, and the grocer all running after.

Next they came to a candy store. And the Elephant said to the Bad Baby, "Would you like a lollipop?" And the Bad Baby said, "Yes."

So the Elephant stretched out his trunk and took a lollipop for himself and a lollipop for the Bad Baby and they went rumpeta, rumpeta, rumpeta, all down the road, with the ice-cream man, and the pork butcher, and the baker, and the snack shop man, and the grocer, and the lady from the candy store all running after.

Next they came to a fruit store. And the Elephant said to the Bad Baby, "Would you like an apple?" And the Bad Baby said, "Yes."

So the Elephant stretched out his trunk and took an apple for himself and an apple for the Bad Baby, and they went rumpeta, rumpeta, rumpeta, all down the road, with the ice-cream man, and the pork butcher, and the baker, and the snack shop man, and the grocer, and the lady from the candy store, and the fruit store man all running after.

Then the Elephant said to the Bad Baby, "But you haven't once said please!" And then he said, "You haven't ONCE said please!"

Then the Elephant sat down suddenly in the middle of the road and the Bad Baby fell off.

And the ice-cream man, and the pork butcher, and the baker, and the snack shop man, and the grocer, and the lady from the candy store, and the fruit store man all went BUMP into a heap.

And the Elephant said, "But he never once said please!"

And the ice-cream man, and the pork butcher, and the baker, and the snack shop man, and the grocer, and the lady from the candy store, and the fruit store man all picked themselves up and said, "Just fancy that! He never *once* said please!"

And the Bad Baby said: "PLEASE! I want to go home to my Mother!"

So the Elephant stretched out his trunk, and picked up the Bad Baby and put him on his back, and they went rumpeta, rumpeta, rumpeta, all down the road, with the ice-cream man, and the pork butcher, and the baker, and the snack shop man, and the grocer, and the lady from the candy store, and the fruit store man all running after.

When the Bad Baby's Mother saw them, she said, "Have you all come for tea?" And they all said, "Yes, *please!*"

So they all went in and had tea, and the Bad Baby's Mother made pancakes for everybody.

Then the Elephant went rumpeta, rumpeta, rumpeta, all down the road, with the ice-cream man, and the butcher, and the baker, and the snack shop man, and the grocer, and the lady from the candy store, and the fruit store man all running after.

But the Bad Baby went to bed.

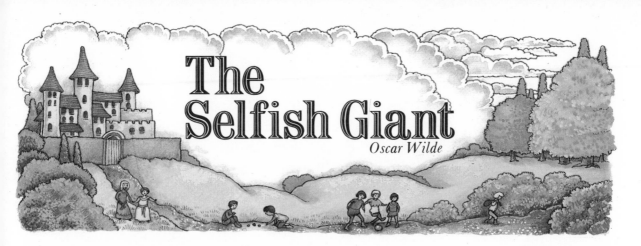

The Selfish Giant
Oscar Wilde

Every afternoon, as they were coming from school, the children used to go and play in the Giant's garden.

It was a large lovely garden, with soft green grass. Here and there over the grass stood beautiful flowers like stars, and there were twelve peach trees that in the springtime broke out into delicate blossoms of pink and pearl, and in the fall bore rich fruit. The birds sat on the trees and sang so sweetly that the children used to stop their games in order to listen to them. "How happy we are here!" they cried to each other.

One day the Giant came back. He had been to visit his friend the Cornish ogre, and had stayed with him for seven years. After the seven years were over he had said all that he had to say, for his conversation was limited, and he determined to return to his own castle. When he arrived he saw the children playing in the garden.

"What are you doing here?" he cried in a very gruff voice, and the children ran away.

"My own garden is my own garden," said the Giant; "anyone can understand that, and I will allow nobody to play in it but myself." So he built a high wall all around it, and put up a notice-board,

TRESPASSERS WILL BE PROSECUTED

He was a very selfish giant.

The poor children now had nowhere to play. They tried to play in the road, but the road was very dusty and full of hard stones, and they did not like it. They used to wander around the high walls when their lessons were over, and talk about the beautiful garden inside. "How happy we were there!" they said to each other.

Then the spring came, and all over the country there were little blossoms and little birds. Only in the garden of the Selfish Giant it was still winter. The birds did not care to sing in it as there were no children, and the trees forgot to blossom. Once a beautiful flower put its head out from the grass, but when it saw the notice-board it was so sorry for the children that it slipped back into the ground again and went off to sleep. The only people who were pleased were the Snow and the Frost.

"Spring has forgotten this garden," they cried, "so we will live here all the year round."

The Snow covered up the grass with her great white cloak, and the Frost painted all the trees silver. Then they invited the North wind to stay with them, and he came. He was wrapped in furs, and he roared all day about the garden, and blew the chimney-pots down. "This is a delightful spot," he said. "We must ask the Hail on a visit." So the Hail came. Every day for three hours he rattled on the roof of the castle till he broke most of the slates, and then he ran round and round the garden as fast as he could. He was dressed in gray, and his breath was like ice.

"I cannot understand why
the Spring is so late in coming," said
the Selfish Giant, as he sat at the
window and looked out at his cold,
white garden; "I hope there will be
a change in the weather."

But the Spring never came, nor the Summer. The Fall
gave golden fruit to every garden, but to the Giant's garden she
gave none. "He is too selfish," she said. So it was always Winter
there, and the North Wind and the Hail, and the Frost, and the
Snow danced about through the trees.

One morning the Giant was lying awake in bed when he
heard some lovely music. It sounded so sweet to his ears that he
thought it must be the King's musicians passing by. It was really
only a little linnet singing outside his window, but it was so long
since he had heard a bird sing in his garden that it seemed to him
to be the most beautiful music in the world. Then the Hail
stopped dancing over his head, and the North Wind
stopped roaring, and a delicious perfume came to him
through the open casement. "I believe the Spring has
come at last," said the Giant; and he jumped out of bed
and looked out.

What did he see?

He saw a most wonderful sight. Through a little hole in the wall the children had crept in, and they were sitting in the branches of the trees. In every tree that he could see there was a little child. And the trees were so glad to have the children back again that they had covered themselves with blossom, and were waving their arms gently above the children's heads. The birds were flying about and twittering with delight, and the flowers were looking up through the green grass and laughing.

It was a lovely scene, only in one corner it was still winter. It was the farthest corner of the garden, and in it was standing a little boy. He was so small that he could not reach up to the branches of the tree, and he was wandering all round it, crying bitterly. The poor tree was still covered with frost and snow, and the North Wind was blowing and roaring above it. "Climb up! little boy," said the Tree, and it bent its branches down as low as it could; but the boy was too tiny.

And the Giant's heart melted as he looked out, "How selfish I have been!" he said; "now I know why the Spring would not come here. I will put that poor little boy on the top of the tree, and then I will knock down the wall, and my garden shall be the children's playground for ever and ever." He was really very sorry for what he had done.

So he crept downstairs and opened the front door quite softly, and went out into the garden. But when the children saw him they were so frightened that they all ran away, and the garden became winter again. Only the little boy did not run, for his eyes were so full of tears that he did not see the Giant coming. And the Giant stole up behind him and took him gently in his hand, and put him up into the tree. And the tree broke at once into blossom, and the birds came and sang on it, and the little boy stretched out his two arms and flung them around the Giant's neck, and kissed him. And the other children when they saw that the Giant was not wicked any longer, came running back, and with them came the Spring, "It is your garden now, little children," said the Giant, and he took a great ax and knocked down the wall. And when the people were going to market at twelve o'clock they found the giant playing with the children in the most beautiful garden they had ever seen.

All day long they played, and in the evening the children came to the Giant to bid him good-bye.

"But where is your little companion?" he said; "the boy I put into the tree." The Giant loved him best because he had kissed him.

"We don't know," answered the children: "he has gone away."

"You must tell him to be sure and come tomorrow," said the Giant. But the children said that they did not know where he lived, and had never seen him before; and the Giant felt very sad.

Every afternoon, when school was over, the children played with the Giant. But the little boy whom the Giant loved was never seen again. The Giant was very kind to all the children, yet he longed for his first little friend, and often spoke of him. "How I would like to see him!" he used to say.

Years went over, and the Giant grew very old and feeble. He could not play about any more, so he sat in a huge armchair, and watched the children at their games, and admired his garden. "I have many beautiful flowers," he said; "but the children are the most beautiful flowers of all."

One winter morning he looked out of his window as he was dressing. He did not hate the Winter now, for he knew it was merely the Spring asleep, and that the flowers were resting.

Suddenly he rubbed his eyes in wonder and looked and looked. It certainly was a marvelous sight. In the farthest corner of the garden was a tree quite covered with lovely white blossoms. Its branches were golden, and silver fruit hung down from them, and underneath it stood the little boy he had loved.

Downstairs ran the Giant in great joy, and out into the garden. He hastened across the grass, and came near to the child. And when he came quite close his face grew red with anger, and he said, "Who hath dared to wound thee?" For on the palms of the child's hands were the prints of two nails, and the prints of two nails were on the little feet.

"Who hath dared to wound thee?" cried the Giant; "tell me that I may take my big sword and slay him."

"Nay," answered the child: "but these are the wounds of Love."

"Who art thou?" said the Giant, and a strange awe fell on him and he knelt before the little child.

And the child smiled on the Giant, and said to him, "You let me play once in your garden, today you shall come with me to my garden, which is Paradise."

And when the children ran in that afternoon, they found the Giant lying dead under the tree, all covered with white blossoms.

Sleeping Beauty

There once lived a king and queen who had no children, which made them very sad. Then one day, to the queen's delight, she found she was going to have a baby. She and the king looked forward with great excitement to the day of the baby's birth.

When the time came, a lovely daughter was born and they arranged a large party for her Christening. As well as lots of other guests, they invited twelve fairies, knowing they would make wishes for their little daughter, the princess.

At the Christening party, the guests and the fairies all agreed that the princess was a beautiful baby. One fairy wished on her the gift of Happiness, another Beauty, others Health, Contentment, Wisdom, Goodness . . . Eleven fairies had made their wishes when suddenly the doors of the castle flew open and in swept a thirteenth fairy. She was furious that she had not been invited to the Christening party, and as she looked around a shiver ran down everyone's spine. They could feel she was evil. She waved her wand over the baby's cradle and cast a spell, not a wish.

"On her sixteenth birthday," she hissed "the princess will prick herself with a spindle. And she will die." With that a terrible hush fell over the crowd.

The twelfth fairy had still to make her wish and she hesitated. She had been going to wish the gift of Joy on the baby but now she wanted to stop the princess dying on her sixteenth birthday. Her magic was not strong enough to break the wicked spell but she tried to weaken the evil. She wished that the princess would fall asleep for a hundred years instead of dying.

Over the years the princess grew into the happiest, kindest and most beautiful child anyone had ever seen. It seemed as though all the wishes of the first eleven fairies had come true. The king and queen decided they could prevent the wicked fairy's spell from working by making sure that the princess never saw a spindle.

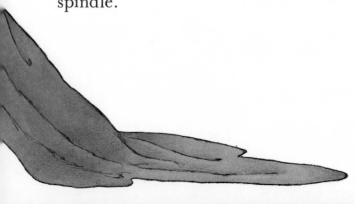

So they banned all spinning from the land. All the flax and wool in their country had to be sent elsewhere to be spun. On their daughter's sixteenth birthday they held a party for the princess in their castle. They felt sure this would protect her from the danger of finding a spindle on her sixteenth birthday.

People came from far and wide to the grand birthday ball for the princess and a magnificent feast was laid out. After all the guests had eaten and drunk as much as they wanted and danced in the great hall, the princess asked if they could all play hide-and-seek, which was a favorite game from her childhood. It was agreed the princess should be the first to hide, and she quickly sped away.

The princess ran to a far corner of the castle and found herself climbing a spiral staircase in a turret she did not remember ever visiting before. "They will never find me here," she thought as she crept into a little room at the top. There to her surprise she found an old woman dressed in black, sitting on a chair spinning.

"What are you doing?" questioned the princess as she saw the spindle twirling, for she had never seen anything like it in her whole life.

"Come and see, pretty girl," replied the old lady. The princess watched fascinated as she pulled the strands of wool from the sheep's fleece on the floor, and twirling it deftly with her fingers fed it on to the spindle.

"Would you like to try?" she asked cunningly.

With all thoughts of hide-and-seek gone, the princess sat down and took the spindle. In a flash she pricked her thumb and even as she cried out, she fell down as though dead. The wicked fairy's spell had worked.

So did the twelfth good fairy's wish. The princess did not die, but fell into a deep deep sleep. The spell worked upon everyone else in the castle too. The king and queen slept in their chairs in the great hall. The guests dropped off to sleep as they went through the castle looking for the princess.

In the kitchen the cook fell asleep as she was about to box the pot boy's ears and the scullery maid nodded off as she was plucking a chicken. All over the castle a great silence descended.

As the years went by a thorn hedge grew up around the castle. Passers-by asked what was behind the hedge, but few people remembered the castle where the king and queen had lived with their lovely daughter. Sometimes curious travelers tried to force their way through, but the hedge grew so thickly that they soon gave up.

One day, many many years later, a prince came by. He asked, like other travelers, what was behind the thorn hedge, which was very tall and thick by now. An old man told him a story he had heard about a castle behind the thorns, and the prince became curious. He decided to cut his way through the thorns. This time the hedge seemed to open out before his sword and in a short while the prince was inside the grounds. He ran across the gardens and through an open door into the lovely old castle.

Everywhere he looked – in the great hall, in the kitchens, in the corridors and on the staircases – he saw people asleep. He passed through many rooms until he found himself climbing a winding stair to an old turret. There in a small room at the top he found himself staring in wonder at the most beautiful girl he had ever seen. She was so lovely that without thinking he leaned forward and gently kissed her.

As his lips touched her, the princess began to stir and she opened her eyes. The first thing she saw was a handsome young man. She thought she must be dreaming, but she looked again and saw he was really there. As she gazed at him she fell in love.

They came down the turret stairs together and found the whole castle coming back to life. In the great hall the king and queen were stretching and yawning, puzzled over how they could have dropped off to sleep during their daughter's party. Their guests too were shaking their heads, rubbing their eyes, and wondering why they felt so sleepy. In the kitchen, the cook boxed the ears of the pot boy, and the scullery maid continued to pluck the chicken. Outside horses stamped and neighed in their stables, dogs barked in the yards, while in the trees birds who had stayed silent for so long burst into song. The hundred year spell had been broken.

The princess told her parents how much she loved the handsome young man who had kissed her, and they were delighted to find he was a prince from a neighboring country. The king gave them his blessing and a grand wedding was arranged.

At the wedding party the princess looked more beautiful than ever, and the prince loved her more every moment. The twelve good fairies who had come to her Christening were invited once again and were delighted to see the happiness of the prince and princess. Towards evening the newly married pair rode off together to their new home in the prince's country, where they lived happily ever after.

Rapunzel

A long time ago, a husband and wife lived happily in a cottage at the edge of a wood. But one day the wife fell ill. She could eat nothing and grew thinner and thinner. The only thing that could cure her, she believed, was a strange herb that grew in the beautiful garden next to their cottage. She begged her husband to find a way into the garden and steal some of this herb, which was called rapunzel.

Now this garden belonged to a wicked witch, who used it to grow herbs for her spells. One day, she caught the husband creeping into her garden. When he told her what he had come for, the witch gave him some rapunzel, but she made him promise to give her their first-born child in return. The husband agreed, thinking that the witch would soon forget the promise. He took the rapunzel back to his wife, who felt better as soon as she had eaten it.

A year later, a baby girl was born and the witch *did* come and take her away. She told the couple they would be able to see their daughter in the garden behind their house. Over the years they were able to watch her grow up into a beautiful child, with long fair hair. The witch called her Rapunzel after the plant her father had come to take.

When she was twelve years old, the witch decided to lock Rapunzel up in a high tower in case she tried to run away. The tower had no door or staircase, but Rapunzel was quite happy up there as she could sit at the window watching the life of the forest and talking to the birds. Yet sometimes she would sigh, for she longed to be back in the beautiful garden where she could run and skip in the sunshine. Then she would sing to cheer herself up.

Each day, the witch came to see her, bringing fresh food. She would stand at the bottom of the tower and call out,

"Rapunzel, Rapunzel, let down your long hair."

Rapunzel, whose long golden hair was plaited, would twist it round one of the bars and drop it out of the window, and the witch would climb up it. When she left, Rapunzel would let down her golden hair again, and the witch would slide nimbly down to the ground.

One day, the king's son was riding through the forest when he heard Rapunzel singing. Mystified, he rode to the tower, but could see no door, so could not understand how anyone could be there. He decided to stay and watch the tower and listen to the singing. After a while the witch came along and the prince watched her carefully. To his amazement, as she called out,

"Rapunzel, Rapunzel, let down your long hair," a long golden plait of hair fell almost to the ground.

The prince saw the witch climb up the hair and disappear through the window, and he made up his mind he would wait until she had gone and see if he could do the same.

So after the witch had gone, he stood where the witch had been and called,

"Rapunzel, Rapunzel, let down your long hair."

When the golden plait came tumbling down, he climbed up as the witch had done and found to his astonishment the most beautiful girl he had ever seen. They talked for a long time and then the prince left, promising to come again. Rapunzel looked forward to his visits, for she had been lonely. He told her all about the world outside her tower, and they fell deeply in love.

One day Rapunzel said to the witch, "Why is it when you climb up my hair you are so heavy? The handsome prince who comes is much lighter than you." At this, the witch flew into a rage and took Rapunzel out of the tower and led her deep into the forest to a lonely spot, and told her she must stay there without food or shelter. The witch cut off Rapunzel's hair and then hurried back to the tower with the long plait of golden hair.

That evening when the prince came by, he called out as usual, "Rapunzel, Rapunzel, let down your long hair."

The witch, who had secured the plait of golden hair inside the window, threw it down. The prince climbed up eagerly, only to be confronted with the wicked witch. "Aha," she cackled, "so you are the visitor who has been coming to see my little Rapunzel. I will make sure you won't see her again," and she tried to scratch out his eyes.

The prince jumped out of the high window, but was not killed for he landed in a clump of thorny bushes. His face, however, was badly scratched and his eyes hurt so that he could not see, and he stumbled off blindly into the forest.

After several days of wandering and suffering, he heard a voice singing. Following the sound, he drew closer and realized he had found Rapunzel, who was singing as she worked to make a home for herself in the forest. He ran towards her, calling her name, and she came and kissed him. As she did so, his eyes were healed and he could see again.

The prince took Rapunzel to his father's palace, where he told his story. Rapunzel was reunited with her parents and a proclamation was made banning the witch from the kingdom. Then a grand wedding took place. Rapunzel married the prince and lived with him for many years. As for the witch, she was never seen again.

The Little Red Hen

Once upon a time there was a little red hen. She lived with a pig, a duck and a cat. They all lived in a house which the little red hen kept clean and tidy. The others never helped. Although they said they meant to, they were all far too lazy. The pig liked to grunt in the mud outside, the duck used to swim in the pond all day, and the cat enjoyed lying in the sun, purring.

One day the little red hen found a grain of wheat.

"Who will plant this grain of wheat?" she asked.

"Not I," grunted the pig from his muddy patch in the garden.

"Not I," quacked the duck from her pond.

"Not I," purred the cat from his place in the sun.

So the little red hen found a nice bit of earth, scratched it with her feet and planted the grain of wheat.

During the summer the grain of wheat grew. First it grew into a tall green stalk, then it ripened in the sun until it had turned a lovely golden color.

"Who will help me cut the wheat?" asked the little red hen.

"Not I," grunted the pig from his muddy patch in the garden.

"Not I," quacked the duck from her pond.

"Not I," purred the cat from his place in the sun.

"Very well then, I will cut it myself," said the little red hen. Carefully she cut the stalk and took out all the grains of wheat from the husks.

"Who will take the wheat to the mill, so that it can be ground into flour?" asked the little red hen.

"Not I," grunted the pig from his muddy patch in the garden.

"Not I," quacked the duck from her pond.

"Not I," purred the cat from his place in the sun.

So the little red hen took the wheat to the mill herself, and asked the miller to grind it into flour.

In time the miller sent a little bag of flour down to the house where the little red hen lived with the pig and the duck and the cat.

"Who will help me to make the flour into bread?" asked the little red hen.

"Not I," grunted the pig from his muddy patch in the garden.

"Not I," quacked the duck from her pond.

"Not I," purred the cat from his place in the sun.

"Very well," said the little red hen. "I shall make the bread myself." She mixed the flour into dough. She kneaded the dough and put it into the oven to bake.

Soon there was a lovely smell of hot fresh bread. It filled all the corners of the house and wafted out into the garden. The pig came into the kitchen from his muddy patch in the garden, the duck came in from the pond and the cat left his place in the sun. When the little red hen opened the oven door the dough had risen up and had turned into the nicest, most delicious looking loaf of bread any of them had seen.

"Who is going to eat this bread?" asked the little red hen.

"I will," grunted the pig.

"I will," quacked the duck.

"I will," purred the cat.

"Oh no, you won't," said the little red hen. "I planted the seed, I cut the wheat, I took it to the mill to be made into flour, and I made the bread, all by myself. I shall now eat the loaf all by myself."

The pig, the duck and the cat all stood and watched as the little red hen ate the loaf all by herself. It was delicious and she enjoyed it, right to the very last crumb.

Hansel and Gretel

There was once a woodcutter who lived with his children at the edge of the forest. He had a son called Hansel and a daughter called Gretel. The children's mother had died when they were small, and as their father had married again they had a step-mother. The family was very very poor indeed. Although the woodcutter worked as hard as he could, he did not earn much money and the whole family often went to bed hungry.

The children's stepmother was not at all fond of Hansel and Gretel. She hated having to make what little food there was go round four people. Often she used to suggest sending the children away, but as their father loved them he always refused.

However, one winter when the family had even less food than usual, the stepmother persuaded her husband to take the children with them deep into the forest. She planned that once they were there she and their father would pretend to go and look for firewood. But in fact they would go home, leaving the children in the forest. Reluctantly the children's father agreed.

The children upstairs in bed had not been able to go to sleep because they were still so hungry. They overheard their father and stepmother talking and Gretel began to cry.

"Don't worry, little sister," said Hansel, "I will look after you." When his father and stepmother had gone to bed he slipped outside and saw some pebbles shining white in the moonlight. Quickly he filled his pockets with these and crept back to bed.

The next morning their father told Hansel and Gretel that they were all going to the forest to collect firewood, and perhaps find some nuts for their supper. They set off together into the forest. As his father led them down first one path and then another, Hansel lagged behind and dropped pebbles from his pocket to mark the paths they walked along. When they reached a part of the forest so far from home that neither Hansel nor Gretel had been there before, the stepmother suggested the children should wait by a tree while she and their father went a little further. Hansel and Gretel were exhausted by the long walk, and sat down thankfully. In no time at all they were fast asleep.

When they awoke, they found the grown-ups had not returned. Gretel cried because she was frightened but Hansel told her how he had dropped pebbles on the paths they had come down, and how when the moon rose his pebbles would gleam in the moonlight and show them the way home. It was just as he said. As the moon shone through the trees, Hansel and Gretel were able to retrace their steps through the forest.

It was nearly dawn when they reached their home. Their father was delighted to see his children again and gave them both a big hug. The stepmother pretended to be cross with them for getting lost. But secretly she was furious that her plan to get rid of the children had failed.

As the days went by there was even less food to eat. Once more the stepmother persuaded her husband to take the children into the forest and leave them there.

"Perhaps they'll die," she said "but at least we won't have to worry about food for them."

Hansel again overheard this plan. This time he was unable to get out and pick up pebbles as the door was locked and barred. Instead at breakfast the next morning, he hid his crust of bread in his pocket.

As the woodcutter and his family set off into the forest, Hansel lingered behind as before and dropped crumbs where the paths divided. He planned to use them just like the pebbles to find the way home. Later the children were left to wait by a tree but their father and stepmother never returned for them. Hansel again comforted Gretel.

"We'll find our way by following the breadcrumbs I've dropped," he told her.

Once more they set out hand in hand, sure that they would be home before morning. But this time they could not find any of Hansel's markers. It was a cold winter. The birds were hungry too, and they had flown down to eat the crumbs that Hansel had dropped. Soon the children realized they were hopelessly lost in the depths of the forest and they both felt very unhappy.

They wandered for two days, hungry and frightened. Then they came suddenly to a clearing and there before them stood a pretty little house. They went closer and saw the walls were made of gingerbread, the roof of fruitcake, and the shining windows of barley sugar. Quickly the children broke bits off the house and pushed the food into their mouths. They noticed that the whole cottage was made of delicious things to eat.

"Hallo, my pretty children," said a voice behind them. "I see I have visitors. Won't you come in and join me for supper?"

The children did not know that a witch was speaking to them as they had come under her spell when they started to eat the little house. She took them indoors and gave them a wonderful meal. Then she showed them to some little white beds and soon Hansel and Gretel were fast asleep.

During the night the wicked witch took Hansel while he was asleep and locked him in a cage. In the morning Gretel found a hard crust waiting for her for breakfast and much heavy work to be done. The witch planned to fatten up Hansel, then eat him. Poor Gretel had to work harder and harder with very little to eat.

Each day the witch would pinch Hansel to see if he was plump enough to make a good meal. She was very shortsighted though, so when Hansel pushed a chicken bone without any meat on it towards her instead of his finger, the witch did not notice. Hansel grew fatter and fatter but he managed to pass some food to Gretel who was treated very cruelly by the witch. Both children longed to escape, but Gretel promised never to run away without her brother.

One day the witch grew impatient. She decided she could wait no longer. She would kill Hansel that very day, and cook him in her big oven.

"Light the fire under the oven, girl!" she ordered. "Heap up the wood and make the oven really hot."

The witch rubbed her hands together. "Test the heat now," she cackled, meaning to roast Gretel first.

But the little girl was clever. "Please show me what to do. Does my head go first?"

"Stupid!" said the witch, "You put your head inside like this."

At once Gretel gave her a big push. The witch went into the oven. Gretel slammed the oven door shut and that was the end of the witch.

Quickly Gretel found the witch's keys and unlocked the cage to let Hansel out. Then they filled their pockets with gold and silver and precious stones. Taking some food as well for the journey, they set off to find their way home.

After wandering for some time they found themselves on a path they knew. Following this they soon found they were near their own home. They ran to the house and burst through the door. There they found their father sitting sadly all alone. Their stepmother had died. He was so pleased to see his children again and they danced around with joy.

"I'll never be so unkind again," he said. "We'll share everything, even a crust."

Then the children emptied their pockets. Their father stared in amazement at the riches they had returned with. Now they had plenty of money and they would never be hungry again.

On a winter's evening the woodcutter loved to sit by the fire and listen to Hansel and Gretel as they told him the story of how they outwitted the wicked witch. And so the three of them lived happily together in the forest for many years.

The Three Wishes

One day a poor woodcutter was working in the forest chopping down trees and sawing them into logs. He stopped for a moment and saw a fairy sitting on a leaf nearby. He closed his eyes, he rubbed them, but she was still there.

"I have come," she told him, "to give you three wishes. The next three wishes you make will come true. Use them wisely." With that she vanished.

After work, the woodcutter returned home and told his wife what had happened. She did not believe a word he said.

"You've just dreamed it," she laughed. "Still, just in case, you'd better think carefully before you wish."

Together they wondered. Should they wish for gold, jewels, a fine home? They argued and disagreed about everything until the woodcutter shouted crossly,

"I'm hungry after all my work. Let's eat first."

"I'm afraid there's only soup," his wife replied. "I'd no money to buy any meat."

"Soup again!" grumbled the woodcutter. "How I wish that we had a fine fat sausage to eat tonight."

Before they could blink, a fine fat sausage appeared on their kitchen table.

"You idiot!" screeched his wife. "Now you've wasted one of our precious wishes. You make me so angry." She went on scolding until he could stand it no more and he shouted,

"I wish that sausage was on the end of your nose!"

Immediately the large sausage jumped in the air and attached itself to the wife's nose. There she stood at the table with the big fat sausage hanging down in front of her. It was difficult to talk with it hanging there and she became really angry when the woodcutter laughed at her because she looked so ridiculous. She pulled and pulled; he pulled and pulled. But the sausage stayed there, stuck on the end of her nose.

The woodcutter soon stopped laughing when he remembered they only had one of the fairy's wishes left.

"Let's wish," he said quickly, "for all the riches in the world."

"What good would that do," she asked, "with a long sausage hanging from my nose? I could not enjoy them for one minute! People would laugh at me wherever I went."

The woodcutter and his wife finally agreed that they could do nothing except get rid of that sausage-nose.

The woodcutter wished and in a flash the sausage was gone, and he and his wife sat down to eat the soup that she had prepared for their supper. The only point they could agree on for a long while was how foolish they had both been to use the fairy's wishes so unwisely. They also wished – too late by now – that they had eaten the sausage when it had first appeared.

The Kings of the Broom Cupboard

Margaret Mahy

A family had once moved into a different house. It was just a small family–a mother, a father and a little girl called Sarah. Well, this house was not exactly new – in fact, it was one of those big old houses full of space and echoes. Footsteps sounded loud and doors shut like guns going off. The family were all a bit nervous of this different house, and felt it was always watching them, waiting to surprise them. Some of the furniture was inside and some was still coming along in the van, but the inside furniture looked nervous too, probably afraid that its people would go and leave it with no one to dust it or sweep beneath it.

The mother was making lunch when Sarah came and said, "Mummy, you know that big closet in the hall?"

"Yes," said the mother, "that's a broom closet."

"Well, there's a king in it, Mummy. He's been shut in there for years and years."

"That's a pity," said the mother. "Why doesn't he come out?"

"He can't!" said Sarah. "He's enchanted. Spiders have spun all over him, Mummy."

"Poor king!" said the mother.

"Poor king!" repeated Sarah. Then she thought for a while and said, "Why don't you rescue him, Mummy?"

"I promise I would if I knew how to do it," the mother replied.

"I'll go and ask how," said Sarah and off she went.

Her mother made some sandwiches and cut some cake before Sarah came back.

"You've just got to unlock the door and the king and his friends will come out," she told her mother.

"What? Is it locked?" asked her mother, surprised. "Then how do you know there's a king in there?"

"I heard him whispering to be let out," Sarah said. "There's a draught under the broom closet door and that king's got a sore throat. He's had it for years. He can only whisper and rustle. I tried to look through the keyhole, but it was too dark to see anything."

"All joking aside," said the mother, who did not believe in the king for one whispering, rustling moment. "I wonder if we have the key for that door." She took up a key ring from the bench and started looking at the keys. "This is for the back door, this is for the front door, this is for the room at the end of the hall."

"A witch enchanted the king," Sarah told her mother. "The king and his friends were just having a picnic when, bang, for no reason at all, this witch enchanted them. Then she built a closet around them. Then she built a house around the closet – this house. That's how it got there. And then that witch just stood there, laughing in a nasty way. Have you found the key?"

"No, there doesn't seem to be any key here," said the mother. Sarah looked worried.

"There should be!" she cried. "The king says today is the day he is to come out."

"He'll have to wait until I find the key," said the mother.

But at that moment a blue pigeon flew into the room. It settled on the table and dropped a tiny black key onto the mother's bread-and-butter plate. Then it cooed in a conceited fashion and did a conceited dance, before it flew out of the window again.

"I told you!" Sarah cried. "It's all working out. That's the key!"

"Well, what a thing to happen!" said the mother. "I wonder if it is the key to the broom closet," and she went into the hall to find out. Sarah ran with her.

As her mother jiggled the key in the lock, Sarah called encouragingly, "Are you there, King? Are you listening? It won't be a moment now."

"I'm afraid the keyhole has rusted up," said the mother sadly. "The king will have to wait."

But at that very moment there came a small clinking and clanking, and four mice came down the hall dragging an oil can. They dropped it at Sarah's feet and ran back to their holes.

"That's useful," said the mother, though she was frowning a bit at the thought of mice in the house. She picked up the oil can and oiled, first the key and then the keyhole.

The key turned easily.

Out from the cupboard came a light like sunshine, the smell of flowers and tomato sandwiches and the sound of drums and trumpets. Out came not one, but seven kings in purple and gold. Out came a whole procession of dancing people in green dresses with flowers in their hair, out came a whole herd of silver deer, strutting white peacocks and a pink elephant with a rose tied to its tail.

Last of all came a witch, dragging a broom after her.

She looked at Sarah and her mother crossly.

137

"I enchanted myself into that broom closet by accident," she muttered. "A wrong word in the wrong place . . . ."

The kings and the queens, the green people, the silver deer, the white peacocks and the pink elephant went down the hall in a sort of parade and a sort of dance. They went one step grave and one step gay, out into the lovely summer day, off through the overgrown garden and then into the trees. Their colors shone, flashed and were lost.

The witch threw the broom back into the closet.

"Get in there where you belong!" she snarled. "No more enchanting for me. I've had a change of heart." She called to the kings, "Wait for me!" Then she went scuttling after them like a mud-colored mouse.

The mother stared after her quite amazed. After a moment she opened the broom closet door and peered uncertainly in.

"There's just that broom left," she said. But the broom went hopping out on its stumpy, bumpy handle, right down the hall, across the garden and into the wood chasing after the witch and the kings.

"Now it's empty," Sarah said with a sigh of satisfaction. "There's room for our own brooms. They should be happy there – it's a nice closet. It's good when enchantments work out properly and there's a happy ending."

From somewhere outside came the echoes of trumpets and drums as the kings of the broom closet went on their way to wherever they were going.

Rumpelstiltskin

One day a king was riding through a village in his kingdom when he heard a woman singing,

"My daughter has burned five cakes today,
My daughter has burned five cakes today."

It was the miller's wife who was cross with her daughter for being so careless. The king stopped as he wanted to hear her song again. The miller's wife hoped to impress the king so she sang,

"My daughter has spun fine gold today,
My daughter has spun fine gold today."

And she boasted that her daughter could spin straw into gold thread.

The king was greatly impressed.

"If your daughter will spin for me in my palace, I'll give her many presents. I might even make her my queen," he announced.

"What a wonderful chance," muttered the miller's wife under her breath. "We'll all be rich." Then out loud she said, "My daughter will be honored, Your majesty."

The king took the girl back to the palace. He ordered a spinning wheel to be placed in a room filled with straw.

"Spin this into gold by the morning or you will die," he commanded. Left alone, the poor girl wept bitterly. She could not spin straw into gold as her mother had boasted and she could not escape as the king had locked the door firmly behind him.

Suddenly a little man appeared from nowhere. He had a small pointed face and wore elfin clothes in green and brown.

"What will you give me, pretty girl, if I spin this straw into gold for you?" he asked.

"I will give you my necklace," the girl replied, "if you really can help me. Yet how can anyone do this task!"

At once the little man sat down by the spinning wheel. Singing strange songs, he spun all the straw into fine gold thread. Then taking the girl's necklace, with a skip and a hop and a stamp of his foot, he disappeared.

When the king unlocked the room the next morning he was astonished and delighted to see the skeins of golden thread. He sent delicious food to the miller's girl. But that evening he took her to another room with an even bigger pile of straw and a spinning wheel.

"Now spin this into gold," he ordered, "and I shall reward you well. But if you fail I shall chop off your head." He walked out, locking the miller's daughter in behind him.

The poor girl stared at the straw and the spinning wheel. "What can I do now?" she cried, "I cannot turn straw into gold and the king will kill me if I fail."

Suddenly the same little man in elfin clothes stood before her.

"What will you give me this time if I spin your gold for you?"

"I'll give you my bracelet," said the miller's girl for she had nothing else to offer.

At once the little man set the spinning wheel whirring. Singing his weird songs, he quickly turned the straw into golden thread. Before dawn he had finished, and snatching her bracelet he was gone, with a skip and a hop and a stamp of his foot.

The king was delighted the next morning, and sent pretty clothes and good food up to the girl as a reward. "If this girl can really spin gold from straw," he thought greedily, "I shall always be rich if I make her my wife. But in case there is some trick I will try her once more."

So the third night the king took the miller's girl into another room with an even greater pile of straw and a spinning wheel.

"Spin this into gold," he commanded. "If you succeed, I shall marry you and you shall be queen. If you fail your head will be chopped off tomorrow."

Once more, as the girl wept bitterly before the pile of straw and the spinning wheel, the little man appeared from nowhere.

"I see you need my help again," he said. "How will you reward me this time if I save your life?"

"I have nothing to give," the miller's daughter said sadly. "Perhaps you should just go and leave me to my fate."

"Ah!" said the little man, "but if the straw is spun into gold tonight, you will become the queen. Will you promise to give me your first child when it is born?"

"Yes! Yes!" cried the girl. When this time came, she was sure she could save her child somehow.

So the little man sat and twirled the spinning wheel, beating his foot on the floor and singing his strange songs. Then with a skip and a hop and a stamp of his foot, once more he was gone.

The next day the king was delighted to see the gold spun from the huge pile of straw and he kept his promise. The miller's daughter became his wife and queen.

And as queen the miller's daughter forgot all about her promise to the little man. About a year later, a fine son was born, and she was horrified when one day the little man appeared.

"I have come to claim the child you promised me," he said, stamping his foot as he spoke.

The queen pleaded with him to release her from the promise.

"Take my jewels and all this gold," she begged, "only leave me my little son."

The little man saw her tears and said, "Very well. You have three days in which to guess my name. You may have three guesses each night. If you fail on the third night, the baby is mine." Then he vanished.

The queen sent for all her servants and asked them to go throughout the kingdom asking if anyone had heard of the little man and if they knew his name. The first night the little man came she tried some unusual names:

"Is it Caspar?" she asked.

"No!" he said and stamped his foot in delight.

"Is it Balschazzar?"

"No!" he said as he stamped his foot again.

"Is it Melchior?"

"No!" he cried. He stamped his foot and disappeared.

The next evening the queen thought she would try some everyday names. So when he appeared she asked,

"Is your name John?"

"No!" he said with his usual stamp.

"Is it Michael?"

"Is it James?"

"No! No!" he cried, stamping his foot each time. Then with a hop and a skip, triumphantly he disappeared.

The next day the queen was very sad for she could not see how she could guess the little man's name. She felt sure she would lose her baby that night.

The palace servants came back without any news except for one who returned to the palace towards the end of the day. He went straight to the queen and told her that at the very edge of the kingdom, under the mountains, he had seen a little man singing as he danced around a fire.

"What did he sing?" asked the queen breathlessly.

"Today I brew, tomorrow I bake,

Next day the queen's child I'll take.

How glad I am that nobody knows

My name is Rumpelstiltskin."

The queen clapped her hands with joy and rewarded the servant. That night the little man appeared and asked if she had guessed his name.

"Is it Ichabod?"

"No!" he cried with pleasure as he stamped his foot.

"Is it Carl?"

"No!" he shouted as he laughed and stamped his foot.

"Is it . . ." the queen hesitated . . . . "Is it Rumpelstiltskin?"

Now it was the queen's turn to laugh. The little man stamped his foot so hard it went through the floor. He disappeared in a flash and was never seen again.

Theseus and the Minotaur

Theseus is one of the great heroes of Greek legends and there are many stories told of his courage and his brave deeds. He was the son of Aegeus, King of Athens, whose country had been defeated in war by the Cretans, led by King Minos.

After the war, King Aegeus signed a treaty, promising that he would send to the island of Crete seven youths and seven maidens, who would be thrown into the labyrinth under the king's palace. A monster called the Minotaur lived in the labyrinth and it would kill the youths and maidens or else they would die from starvation. Each year there was great grief and sorrow when the seven young men and women were chosen and sent off to Crete.

Theseus was determined to stop this cruel sacrifice. Like everyone else, he hated to think of so many fine young people going off to their death every year. As soon as he was old enough, he insisted on going in place of one of the young men chosen.

The people did their best to stop him, saying that the king's son was needed by his people and that he would never return. His father, the king, pleaded with him until the moment when the boat was ready to sail. Then when he saw nothing could stop Theseus from going, he asked his son to promise one thing.

"If by some miracle you return, Theseus, change these black sails of mourning that are on the ship now to white sails. Every day I shall stand on the cliffs and watch for the ship's return. If the sails are white, I shall come to meet you. If they are black, I will throw myself off the cliffs down to the grey rocks and the sea below. For if you are dead I cannot live any longer."

Theseus promised that if he returned alive the black sails would be changed to white, and so, at last, the ship set sail.

When they arrived in Crete, Theseus asked to see King Minos, and when he was taken before the king he requested that he alone might go to the Minotaur, and that the other Athenians be set free at once. But King Minos refused. Theseus then asked to visit the Minotaur first. If he came away alive then his fellow countrymen should be returned to Athens. Minos agreed to this for he was sure that no one could ever come out of the labyrinth alive. He ordered that Theseus be taken to the labyrinth alone the very next evening.

Now King Minos had a daughter called Ariadne and she listened closely to Theseus as he talked to her father. She fell in love with the young prince and decided to help him. That night Ariadne came in disguise to the prison where the young Athenians were held, and spoke to Theseus. She told him that the Minotaur lived in a cavern at the center of the labyrinth. She feared that Theseus would never find his way out of the labyrinth, for there were countless twists and turns in the passages and hundreds of choices of ways to go. It would be impossible to remember the way out even if he did fight and kill the Minotaur.

"Take this with you," said Ariadne, pressing into Theseus's hand a tiny ball of silken thread. "Let it unwind as you make your way into the labyrinth, and then if you do kill the Minotaur, you will be able to find your way out and escape before my father's guards kill you. When you are out of the labyrinth come down to the bay where your ship will be waiting."

"Who are you?" asked Theseus, "and why are you helping me in this way?"

"I am Ariadne, King Minos's daughter," she replied, "and I have heard many tales of your bravery, Theseus. If you escape the labyrinth I want you to take me away with you, for I am unhappy living here in Crete."

The next evening, the guards came to take Theseus to the Minotaur. They did not notice the knife that Theseus had concealed, nor the ball of silken thread which he started to unwind as soon as the guards left him at the entrance to the labyrinth.

Theseus wandered first down one passage, then down another, and another, and another, until he came at last to a large cavern at the center of the labyrinth. There he paused on hearing a roaring bellowing sound. He tried to accustom his eyes to the dim light so that he could see what his opponent looked like. He had heard fearful stories about the Minotaur but no one had ever been able to describe it. Now, through the gloom, he saw a monstrous figure, half bull, half man. The creature sniffed the air as it smelt the stranger, then with a further bellow of rage, it thundered towards Theseus.

Theseus braced himself for the shock of the monster's charge. He was renowned for his strength and courage and at this moment, he badly needed both. He seized the bull's horns on the Minotaur's head as it charged towards him and he jumped neatly over its back. Again and again the Minotaur came at him, and again and again Theseus turned in time, using all his might to twist the thick neck each time he held the horns. The creature's strength gradually faded as Theseus, the champion wrestler of Athens, landed on his feet first on one side, then the other.

The blood was pounding in Theseus's head and his body ached. At last he twisted the monster's neck one more time as he jumped, and the Minotaur crashed to the ground, gasping.

Theseus quickly pulled the knife from its sheath and plunged it into the Minotaur's heart. He groped for Ariadne's thread at the entrance to the cavern and, keeping his hand on it, he followed it through the labyrinth until he reached the entrance. From there, by the light of the moon, he made his way down to the bay where he found his ship. Ariadne had forced her father's guards to release the other Athenians from prison, and as he climbed on board, the order was given to sail. They knew they must get away from Crete as quickly as possible as King Minos would be swift to avenge the death of the Minotaur.

Theseus found Ariadne waiting on the ship and he was glad to see her there for she was very beautiful. Moreover, now the Minotaur was dead, he had time to think of other things and it was not long before he fell in love with her. The ship sailed to another island called Naxos, where they disembarked and celebrated Theseus's great victory. They feasted and drank wine on Naxos for many days.

At last Theseus decided the time had come to return to Athens and tell his father that the Minotaur was dead and his people need no longer sacrifice seven youths and maidens each year. But Adriadne was happy on the island of Naxos and decided not to leave with Theseus and the other Athenians. So much had happened since leaving Athens that Theseus quite forgot his promise to his father and the ship sailed towards Athens still carrying black sails.

Each day, King Aegeus watched from the cliffs for his son. One morning, he saw the ship on which Theseus had left sail into sight. When he saw the black sails, the old king was overcome with grief at the thought of his son's death. Full of sorrow that he had allowed his son to go to Crete, he threw himself off the cliff down to the sharp gray rocks and churning sea below. To this day that part of the sea is called the Aegean Sea in his honor.

As for Theseus, he came home to a royal funeral, and not to the joyful celebrations he had planned.

The Nightingale

This is a story about an Emperor of China, who was of course Chinese. It happened many many years ago and that is why you should listen – before the story is forgotten.

This Emperor had the most magnificent palace in the world. It was made of porcelain and decorated all over with the most beautiful paintings and the finest ornaments. The palace gardens were splendid too. The flowers in the flower beds were hung with little bells which tinkled in the wind as you walked by. Everything had been done to make the garden as lovely as possible.

The gardens stretched so far that not even the gardeners knew where they ended. Beyond the lawns with their wonderful borders of flowers there were deep lakes and a thick forest.

The forest extended right down to an inlet of the sea where a poor fisherman kept his boat. In the tall trees near the sea, a nightingale sang each night, and when the fisherman heard it, he would exclaim, "Lord, how beautifully she sings!"

Many travelers came to China. They admired the Emperor's palace of porcelain and his magnificent garden with its tinkling flowers, and they marveled at the deep lakes and the forests of lofty trees. But when they heard the nightingale sing, they, like the fisherman, would say, "How very beautiful!" And they would add, "The nightingale is the most beautiful thing of all."

When they returned home, some of them wrote books about their travels. And one of these books was sent as a gift to the Emperor of China by the Emperor of Japan. The Emperor took great pleasure in reading about the splendor of his palace, and he sat in his golden chair and nodded his head with approval as he read and read. But when he came to the part about the nightingale, the Emperor stopped in surprise.

"What nightingale?" he exclaimed. "If it is the most beautiful thing in my empire, why do I not know about it?"

He summoned his Lord Chamberlain, who bowed low and said

"Your Imperial Majesty, do not believe everything that is written in books. It is probably make-believe," for he had never heard of the nightingale himself and did not wish to seem stupid before the Emperor.

But the Emperor told him that all the other things written in the book were true, so the part about the nightingale must be true also. "Find the nightingale," he ordered, "for I should like it to sing before me tonight."

The Lord Chamberlain asked everyone in the palace, but no one had heard of the nightingale, until someone found a little kitchen maid. She said that she had sometimes heard the nightingale singing when she took scraps of food from the palace kitchen to her family in the evening.

"I will show you where she sings," she offered. Followed by half the Emperor's court, she went through the garden and into the forest down towards the sea.

As they walked, a cow began to moo, and all the courtiers fell to their knees, crying, "Listen to the nightingale! How very beautiful it is!" But the maid laughed and told them it was only a cow. As they passed a lake, they heard some frogs croaking, and once more they fell down and cried out with admiration, "Listen to the nightingale! How sweetly it sings!" But the kitchen maid laughed again and told them it was only frogs they had heard.

At last, they came to a clearing and the little kitchen maid pointed to the nightingale sitting in a tree.

"How strange," said the Lord Chamberlain, "that the nightingale should look so drab and shabby. It is a very ordinary bird." But he had to agree that the nightingale's song was the loveliest sound he had ever heard.

"Little nightingale, will you sing for the Emperor?" asked the kitchen maid.

The nightingale, thinking the Emperor must be among this grand company, said, "Of course, your Imperial Highness," and began to sing again. When she had finished, the Lord Chamberlain explained that the Emperor was waiting at the palace where a great reception was to be held, and it was there that the Emperor wished to listen to the nightingale. "I sing better in the open air," said the nightingale, but she agreed to go with them to the palace.

They found the Emperor sitting in the middle of a great hall, with a golden perch beside him where the nightingale was to sing. The courtiers stood around dressed in their finest, most colorful clothes, looking at the little gray bird. As the singing began, the Emperor's eyes filled with tears for he had never heard anything so beautiful in his life.

Tears ran down his cheeks as the nightingale sang one song after another, and the little bird was happy, knowing her songs had reached the Emperor's heart. When the nightingale had finished singing, the Emperor offered his own golden slipper, but the nightingale said, "Thank you, but I have reward enough in seeing the Emperor's tears."

After that night the little bird lived in the Emperor's palace in a golden cage. Twice a day, she was allowed to fly in the garden with twelve silken threads tied to her feet, held by twelve courtiers. The whole city talked of nothing but the wonderful nightingale, and the ladies of the court even put water in their mouths so that they would make a gurgling sound as they talked, like the nightingale's song.

One day a parcel arrived for the Emperor, labeled NIGHTINGALE. When he unwrapped it, he found a beautiful silver and gold nightingale which glittered and sparkled with sapphires, diamonds and rubies. When it was wound up with a little jeweled key, its silver tail went up and down and it sang one of the nightingale's songs. It was a gift from the Emperor of Japan.

Everyone admired the golden nightingale as it sang, first once, then again. Then the Emperor wanted it to sing a duet with the real nightingale, but the real nightingale sang a different song and they did not sound right together. So the court listened to the golden bird while it sang its song thirty-three times.

153

"Now let my real nightingale sing on her own," said the Emperor at last. But when they looked around, the nightingale was gone! No one had noticed her slip out of an open window and fly off to the forest. "How ungrateful!" everyone exclaimed, and the Emperor banished the nightingale from his empire.

The jeweled nightingale delighted everyone at court. It sparkled all the time and it sang so prettily. The Emperor arranged for the people of his city to hear it on the next feast day and the crowds were charmed by its song. Only the poor fisherman was not quite sure.

"It certainly sings a lovely song," he said thoughtfully, "but when I compare it with the real nightingale I feel there is something missing."

One evening when the golden bird was singing its best for the Emperor and his court, there was a *Whirr* and a *B-rrr* and a *Click*, and the nightingale fell silent. All the best doctors were sent for, but in the end it was the watchmaker who mended the bird. He warned the Emperor that the clockwork was wearing out and advised him not to make the bird sing more than once a day. So the Emperor kept it close to his bedside and listened to it once each evening.

Five years passed and the Emperor lay dying. He was all alone, for everyone else was preparing for the announcement of the new Emperor. As he lay cold and pale in his great bed, he felt a weight over his heart and, opening his eyes, he saw the figure of Death bending over him. Death was wearing the Emperor's crown; in one hand he held the Emperor's great golden sword, in the other his beautiful banner. Round him floated strange shadowy faces. They were the Emperor's past good and evil deeds, crowding in on him and calling, "Do you remember . . . .? Do you remember . . . .?" The Emperor shuddered and turned away. Then he saw the clockwork nightingale by his bed.

"I must have music!" he cried, hoping to push away the faces and silence their voices. But there was no one to wind up the nightingale, and it sat silent on its golden perch.

Then suddenly, through the window came an exquisite delicate song. On a tree outside was the real nightingale. She had heard the Emperor's call, and come to sing him songs of comfort and hope. As she sang, the Emperor felt stronger and the shadows started to melt away. Death himself listened and, when the nightingale paused, he said, "Go on, little nightingale, go on!"

"I will only sing again if you will give me the Emperor's golden sword, his banner and his Imperial crown," answered the nightingale, and as she sang Death handed back the treasures. Then the nightingale sang of quiet churchyards where white roses grow, where the grass is wet from the tears of those who mourn. All at once, Death had a great longing to go to his own garden, and he floated out of the window.

"Thank you, thank you, little nightingale," cried the Emperor. "I drove you from my empire, yet you have come back to sing my sins away and take Death from my heart. How shall I repay you?"

"You repaid me," the little bird said, "the very first time I sang to you and drew tears from your eyes. Those are the jewels from the heart that reward a singer. Sleep now, and I will sing to you once more."

As the nightingale sang, the Emperor slept a long and healing sleep. He awoke to find the sun shining through the windows. He was still alone, for his servants thought that he was dead. Only the nightingale was there, outside the window.

"You must always stay with me now," smiled the Emperor, "I shall break that clockwork bird into a thousand pieces."

"Please don't harm it," murmured the nightingale. "It did what it could. As for me, I cannot live in the palace again, but let me come here when I like. Then I will sing to you of those that are happy, of those that are sad, of everything that you cannot see from your palace. A small bird can fly by the poorest fisherman's cottage and the richest house in the land. My songs will make you the wisest of emperors, but one thing you must promise me."

"Anything," replied the Emperor.

"Talk to no one about the little bird who tells you everything."

And so the nightingale flew away. When the servants came in, expecting to see their emperor dead, he stood before them in his royal robes alive and well. And the Emperor turned to them with a smile, and said, "Good Morning!"

The End